BADMAN

A WESTERN NOVEL

Walt Polzin

Walt Polzin

Published in Medford, OR

Copyright 2013 by Walt Polzin.

Reprint 2014

Printed in the United States of America

ISBN 13: 978-1-59977-051-2

ISBN 10: 1-59977-051-2

Library of Congress Catalog Card Number: 2012943714

CONTENTS

"I said draw, Mister." The hulking, unshaven man stood in the middle of the street. He tilted his forehead forward, issuing a look of challenge. "Draw!"

"But I ain't done nothing to you." The man's voice shook. Drops of sweat trickled down his forehead. He obviously knew the other man.

"But I'm gonna do something to you," John Williams said. "I don't like that shirt you're wearing. I'm gonna kill you anyway, so you might as well try to save your yella hide. Now, draw."

"But I—"

John drew his gun and fired.

The dead man's body crumpled to the street, his face frozen in surprise.

"John," said his brother, Al Williams. He shook his head. *Is John ever going to learn?* "Let's go."

"Sorry it took so long. I just wanted to have a little fun before we got down to business." John laughed.

The dead man lying in the street did not draw any notice. The two brothers left him and started up the boardwalk on Main Street, which was empty

"Al, you go around the back, and come in through the back door of the bank. I'll go in here at the front." Since he was always pursuing excitement, it was natural that John would take the more dangerous entrance.

Al went around back of the bank in the little Wyoming town of Lander and then watched as John entered through the front, with his gun drawn.

"Alright, everybody up against the wall," John said.

The people in the bank quickly scurried toward the wall on one side of the room.

"Not you, teller. You grab a money bag and start filling it." John paused and motioned toward Al. "Don't try anything. Brother Al there at the back door would love to put a bullet through you."

Al frowned, but he hoped the bluff would be enough to prevent John from needing to kill again.

Eyes turned toward Al. The sight of his gun was enough to stall any unnecessary movement.

John motioned for the teller to fill the bag. "That's enough," John said after a moment. He turned to Al, "Let's go."

They started for the front door. Al guarded the people in the bank, while John searched the street.

"OK, let's get out of this town," John sneered.

They ran to their horses, which were tied to a post just down the street.

A group of people had gathered around the lifeless body of the man John shot. They looked up from the dead man as John and Al rode past. People from the bank spilled out into the street, shouting that it had been robbed by the Williams brothers.

John and his brother disappeared beyond the edge of town. Everyone knew they would head for their hideout in the mountains, west of town. Yet, no one was anxious to go after them.

The Wind River Mountains held a number of good hiding places. The Williams Gang used one of them for a base. The semi-barren hills gave way to more wooded terrain at the foot of the mountains. Here and there, a gully afforded concealment from distant view.

Half an hour after leaving Lander, John and Al stopped their tired horses in front of two parallel stacks of balanced boulders that formed a natural archway. This was the entrance to their hideout.

John, the bigger of the two men, at six-foot-two, dismounted first and led his horse through the opening. Al followed closely behind. The archway was just wide enough to walk the horses through on foot. Any man who tried to ride his mount through would wind up without any meat on his legs.

Just inside the archway, the rugged terrain sloped and then dropped steeply downhill to a basin. The camp the brothers had built was hidden from view by large, overhanging rocks.

Five minutes after they led their horses down the winding slope, several lean-to structures came into their view, situated around the perimeter of the basin. These structures included a well for their water and a small corral; although, the horses were generally left to wander free. The only way the horses could find nourishment in the dry basin was to forage over as large an area as possible. The camp also contained a storage shed.

Knowing the tired horses weren't likely to attempt to climb back out of the basin, John and Al unsaddled them and carried the saddles to one of the lean-tos. Then, across from each other, at a makeshift table, sitting on two empty kegs, the brothers began to relax and count their haul.

"That's $250 for you and $250 for me." John laid his hands out flat on the table. "Not much for all the trouble. We'll do better on the next one."

Al saw a sparkle in John's eyes that he could not quite understand.

"We'll hit a train next. They're always full of money." John shoved his half of the take into his shirt pocket. "The law will be looking for us, but that'll make it all the more fun."

Fun? How about dangerous? Al didn't voice his opinion. "Why don't we lay off for a while?" He knew that if they didn't, they were going to get caught. "Can't we just go somewhere and enjoy the money we've already got?"

John looked at his brother. "Maybe after this job." *Why is Al always a bundle of nerves? Nobody is gonna stop us from taking what we want.* Reaching into a burlap sack that was lying on the ground, John pulled out a bottle of whiskey. After shooing two flies from glasses he found on one of the lean-to's supports, he blew the dust out of them, poured two shots, and handed one to Al.

The first swig tasted of gritty dirt, but without exchanging any more words, the brothers drank until they had emptied the bottle. The blistering heat and the whiskey knocked them out cold. Neither man awoke before morning.

Since they were not too high in the mountains, summer nights weren't terribly cold, but they were considerably cooler than the days. Thus the morning air was tangy enough to clear the brothers' heads when they awoke.

John got to his feet and starting planning their next heist. "The gold shipment comes out of the mines on Wednesday," he said. "The payroll comes back to the mines on Friday. Gold is too heavy to handle, so I figure the payroll is a better idea."

Al wasn't so quick to get to his feet. He rolled over on his back and listened to John's plans, marveling over his brother's greed.

"We could still use a hand though—it's more than a two person job," John said. "We've got 'til Friday to round up someone."

"Are you sure you want to rob a payroll train?" Al didn't like the way this sounded. "I mean, after that bank job, we've got enough money for a while. We hardly ever spend any anyway. You said yourself that the law will be waiting for us to come down out of the hills. Besides, the payroll will be heavily guarded."

John stared at Al. "You're lucky you're my brother. I wouldn't stand for anyone else talking to me like that."

"I know," Al said. "I remember when you gunned down that man from the Rivera Gang. They aren't going to forget it either." He stood up and looked into John's face. "I know I'm not a lot safer than he was."

Al walked idly around the lean-to, wondering how to slow down his brother and make him see reason. *Why would he start being reasonable now?* "There isn't anyone around here, on either side of the law, with much love for you."

John grinned, obviously enjoying the idea. "Ah, but that's not altogether true. There is someone who likes me." John's smile widened into a sneer.

"Marcia doesn't count," Al said. "She's not going to help us with the robbery."

"Don't bet on it. Marcia'd do just about anything for me, maybe even rob a train." John chuckled.

"But that's not what I mean," Al said. "I mean that you're not going to find anyone who will help with this job, like you want. So, maybe it's not . . . such a good . . . idea."

"Oh, I've got someone in mind." John wiggled his eyebrows at his older brother. "Remember Lan Phelan?"

"The ex-prizefighter?" Al asked.

"That's right. He's camped up toward the Montana border. I heard from an old drifter a while back that since Lan turned outlaw, his fortunes haven't been too good." John paced around the lean-to, stirring up dust with his boots. "What would you expect from an outlaw who doesn't carry a gun?" John snickered. "But even without a gun, I want him. I think he'll join up. He respects me."

Al cringed.

"He has ever since we first met. I don't really know why. I figure if we can catch the train at the wide curve along the river, just as the tracks climb to where the mine spurs are, it'll be moving slow enough for us to get on board without anyone knowing it." John tugged on his cowboy hat. "Once we're on the train, we can't use any guns and risk alerting the crew or passengers, so we have to take out the guards, one at a time, quietly.

Al didn't like the way this sounded. *How are we going to take out all of the guards without anybody hearing or noticing what we are doing?*

"After we get the payroll, you, me, and Lan throw the strong box off the train, jump, and head back to our horses, and then home. Chances are the train will be in the depot before anyone knows what happened. We'll be sitting here with a drink in our hands."

"You want Lan because we can't use our guns and Lan's good with his fists?"

"That's right, little brother. Although I'd much rather kill a couple of guards, even I know that having the fun of raising havoc could make the job impossible. I'm not ready to take on a whole trainload of people. My gun only holds six shots."

Al let out a sigh. "What makes you so sure he'll join us?"

"Lan is always interested in making money if it's his kind of work, and this is just his kind of job. Besides, I just told you, he's down and out. He needs this."

"But what if he won't come with us? Can we forget the train job?" Al was hopeful.

"Not a chance. If he doesn't want in, I'll just ask Marcia." John laughed so hard his stomach shook. He slapped his brother on the back. "What do you say we go find out if he'll join us?"

John didn't notice Al's head wagging as he followed his brother out of the lean-to.

Leaving the hideout was always a risky business, for the same reasons that made it such a safe place for them to hole up. The concealing rock ledge that hid the camp from view also prevented anyone in the basin from seeing what might be lying in wait above in the rocks. The narrow trail meant leading the horses single file, with no cover for safety and no means of a quick escape.

Both brothers knew that if the hideout were ever stumbled upon by the law, it would become a deathtrap for them. Each time they left the hideout, Al wondered if it might be the last time.

For the next couple of days, John and Al rode along a trail heading toward the border of eastern Montana. They picked their way down from the wooded hills to flat lands of the Shoshone Basin, which spread into the dry, rolling hills of Wyoming. They spent the first night of their trip camped southwest of the Bighorn River.

The next day, they crossed the Bighorn River and the Wind River and began climbing the Owl Creek Mountains. Further to the east lay the badlands, but they were headed in a more northerly direction.

The land they crossed was dotted with little streams. But the awe-inspiring scenery failed to move John's emotions. He was concentrating on finding Lan, and that was all.

Three days after the trip started, they found Lan fishing with a crooked branch in a stream that eventually fed into the Wind River.

The gurgling of the stream prevented Lan from noticing the Williams brothers as they approached.

John motioned for Al to dismount quietly. Approaching a man by surprise could be dangerous, but they knew he didn't carry a gun. Al was happy to know that John's wasn't threatening their lives this time.

The sound of the stream grew louder as they approached Lan from behind. "Alright, Lan," John said. "Your time has come. Make a move."

Lan spun around. "I'm unarmed. I'm . . ." Recognition crossed Lan's face.

"You see why you ought to carry a gun, Lan?" John said. "Some mean hombre like me might come along and plug you for the fun of it." John laughed.

Al, who, unlike his brother, had not gotten to know the other man the last time they met, let out a sigh of relief.

Lan patted his chest. "Yeah, but if I carried a gun, I'd probably have a lot more scumbags trying to plug me. Besides, I wouldn't be any good with a gun. I would end up dead anyway." He looked at Al. "Ain't that right, Al? Most men won't shoot an unarmed man. But, of course, that wouldn't stop your brother. So, what difference would a gun make?" He spat at the rocks at the stream's edge.

Al didn't say anything, so Lan went on.

"What brings you two out here? It sure wasn't just to scare me. There ain't nobody else here for you to shoot, and there's nothing here to steal." Lan glared at John.

There was a moment of silence, and then John spoke. "Lan, we're gonna rob a mine payroll train."

Lan tilted his head at the elder Williams brother.

"We want to be real quiet, so you fit in just fine. We want another hand, but not one with a loud gun."

"What makes you think I'm interested?" Lan asked.

"Well, I thought of you because this job could bring in some money for you."

Lan twisted his mouth, as if he was in thought.

"I figured you're pretty tired of a fish diet, if you're lucky enough to have that." John motioned toward the end of Lan's fishing pole, which was lying on the ground. "There's supposed to be bait on a hook at the end of that." John laughed. "There's a good chunk of money in this for you—probably no trouble, just your style. I'll cut you in for a quarter share of the take."

Lan looked absently around for a minute. "What makes you think I'm hard up?"

"Oh, that's just what I heard."

"I suppose I could use a little cash." Lan walked around John and picked up his line. "The quarter cut is OK, but I want something else."

John looked Lan up and down.

"Don't look at me like that. I don't think it's anything you can't live with." Lan backed up a little. "I want to be a permanent partner. I'm tired of being on my own, and I'm tired of being broke. I don't want to get into any bloody massacres, but I could use a little consistency in my income."

John exhaled. *He could be a real asset for jobs like this one, but he could also be a huge liability when guns are blazing.* "Well, bloody massacres are my specialty. Maybe you're not the man I want after all."

"Come on, John. What do you say? I could be good for you. You could use some brains in your outfit."

"Watch yourself." John yanked his gun from his holster.

"Hey," Lan said, "don't panic."

John put his gun away.

Al could not hide his shock at someone wanting to be partners with John. Everyone knew about the Rivera incident. No other outlaw would trust John, and law-abiding citizens and lawmen wanted nothing more than for him to be dead. Now, here was a guy who wanted a permanent partnership. It was hard to believe.

"I'm not sure I like the idea of a partner," John said. "Al and I do alright by ourselves, most of the time." He paused. "Then again, maybe we might do better with an additional man."

Al watched the battle of John's emotions.

"I call the shots," John said.

There was a silent pause. Then Lan nodded affirmatively, his face breaking into a smile.

John thrust out his hand. "Welcome to the Williams Gang, Lan."

The tension was gone.

Lan shook John's hand and turned to Al with a smile on his face and shook his hand. Then Lan took one last look at his un-baited fishing hook and, with a shake of his head, threw the makeshift pole and line into the water. He obviously felt it was time for a much more profitable way of life.

The sun started to set as they made small talk and then began to focus on the details of the robbery. The three men made camp a short distance from the river. John pulled out a bottle of booze from his saddlebags, and the outlaws passed it around. That eventually sent them into slumber land.

The next morning, the groggy men rolled up their bedding and broke camp long after the sun had already risen. Hungry and stiff, they started their trek back to central Wyoming. John would not listen to pleas for a delay for coffee and breakfast. He was anxious to be back to the hideout and prepare for the train robbery.

Two days later, the men started out from the hideout, ready to tackle the Central Pacific.

A short ride from the hideout, the railroad tracks wound up one of the many hills just outside Lander. It was still before noon, and the three members of the Williams Gang were hidden behind jagged rocks that overhung the right of way. The secluded spot offered a scenic view of the river beyond the tracks, where it wandered along the hills. But the scenery, as usual, was of no interest to John.

"Well, I'll be," John said to his companions. "Here it comes, right on schedule."

The steam locomotive was just rounding the curve and starting up the incline. The speed of the train was slowed by the steep grade. Its wheels struggled to keep traction; yet it continued to move forward.

The tender followed the locomotive up the incline. Then came the baggage car. The three outlaws jumped from the rocks onto the roof of that car and spread out for their assigned jobs.

Al struck the roof guard quickly and quietly. He fell from the car and then rolled over the downhill embankment, into the river.

John worked his way cautiously along the side of the car by moving hand over hand on the rain drain rail at the top of the car, searching for a place for his feet at the base of the windows. Eventually, he reached the front end of the baggage car. The doors were open because of the heat of the day. There was no concern about security while the train was underway.

By the time Lan's entrance through the rear door had distracted the two armed guards inside, John had sprung onto the nearer of the two, knocking the guard to the floor. This counter distraction turned the other guard's head just long enough for Lan to deliver a knockout punch to the chin. Within a minute, the struggle was over, and Al joined the others. The train still slowly wound its way up the side of the mountain.

The outlaws spotted the payroll strongbox. Al and Lan each grabbed one handle and headed for the rear door.

John drew his pistol and aimed at one of the fallen guards, intent upon enjoying the man's death.

"John," Al said, "no guns. Remember? Too noisy."

"Oh, yeah, I forgot," John said. He jammed his gun back into his holster. Then he drew his foot back, smiling at Al and Lan, and kicked the man on the floor in the head.

Al and Lan exchanged looks. Then they threw the strongbox clear of the rear door. Their work was done, so the three outlaws jumped from the slow-moving train.

The box survived its landing intact. The outlaws found it lying between the rails and dragged it off the tracks.

"Lan, go back for the horses," John said.

As John and Al watched, the train passed beyond a large rock outcropping and disappeared from sight. The train whistle blew, perhaps to chase an animal from the tracks.

In a few minutes, Lan returned with the horses. The three men lifted the box onto the back of one horse and secured it. Then Al mounted behind John, and all three men rode down the tracks to a clearing, with Lan controlling the loaded horse. Then they changed direction and headed for their hideout. John knew that the guards would be unconscious for some time and even when they awoke it would be difficult for them to alert the engine crew that there had been a problem before the train arrived at the station.

Later, safely back in the basin, the men sat on kegs as John doled out the cash—one-fourth for Lan and the rest for Al and himself.

"It's a shame Marcia can't help spend this." John waved the money in a circular motion.

Al could see he was already thinking of more exciting adventures.

"Who's Marcia?" Lan asked.

"Not now," Al said.

"Well, boys, who do we hit next?" John grinned.

"We've barely even finished counting this money." Al understood his brother's intentions, but he needed to reason with him so they wouldn't get caught. "Why talk about another job now? It'll be safer to pull the next job after things have cooled down."

"Safer? Safer? Al, are you chicken or something? You've been disagreeing with me a lot lately. You're lucky you're my brother. Anyone else would be dead by now." John rose from his seat and stood over Al. It was not unusual for the brothers to come near to blows.

Al rose too. "John, I'm not disagreeing with you. I just don't see any reason to ask for trouble." He tried to stay calm so he wouldn't incite John even more. "By now, the train has reached town, and they know it's been robbed. They'll know it was us. The guards saw us. Why leave here and run the risk of bumping into a posse or something?"

John's face turned red and his right fist smashed into Al's left cheek, sending Al to the ground.

Suddenly, Lan jumped over Al's overturned keg and stood between the two brothers in a crouching position—apparently, ready to engage in his specialty. "Stop it," Lan said.

John's anger turned to rage as he gauged his chances of reaching the table behind Lan, where he'd left his gun while counting the money. John turned back toward his new adversary. "You tired of living or something?" He was thinking of a day when his gun would not be so far from his hand. He would kill Lan—maybe not today, but one day.

Al, who was still on the ground, shuffled back, keeping an eye on his brother.

"The way I see it, we're in this together," Lan said. Stepping between them, he held his hands out in both directions, looking like a boxing referee. "Fighting among ourselves only hurts us. We have to stick together. We're the Williams Gang. I know you would like to kill me. But right now, you're in a position to get the snot beaten out of you, so stop and think about it for a minute." Lan remained silent for a moment, his eyes never leaving John's face.

John knew that if he moved, Lan would fulfill his threat.

"You know my interference was for the good of us all."

Al picked up his overturned keg and sat down on it next to the table. He was watching for John's reaction to Lan's overture. John only continued to glare at Lan.

Al took a chance and changed tactics. "Hey, John, what are you going to get for Marcia with all this loot?"

John looked at his brother in bewilderment and then chuckled a little. Al saw the tension and rage instantly leave John's body. He pulled another keg up to the table and then motioned to Lan. "Come on; sit down."

Lan did as requested.

"You're right," John said. "We are all in this together." He glanced at Al, who got up and dusted himself off. "I won't have much of a gang if I kill you guys." John tilted his head back and laughed.

Al watched John to make sure he wasn't going to go for the gun.

"Al, you're absolutely right," John said. "We don't need more money right now. But what do you say about having a little fun? I'll pick up some nice things for Marcia. I might even pay for 'em. And I'll get a couple of gals for you guys and one for me, and we'll have a party. How's that sound?" John gently lifted his gun from the table and holstered it.

A party meant leaving the hideout. Silently, the knowledge was shared by the two more reasonable members of the gang. They dared not speak out against John, especially at that moment.

Al wondered about John's strange perversions—he had for years. John's continual flaunting of dangerous undertakings was nothing compared to the joy he took in killing, maiming, or ridiculing. Life seemed to mean nothing to John. His only goal was to take from society, and he didn't care who had a problem with his attitude.

John would not be swayed from his plans to party. "OK, it's settled," John said. "I've thought it out. We can go up north, to Montana. The law won't be looking for us there. So, we can do whatever we want, without worrying about drawing attention. You guys satisfied with that? You get a good night's sleep. We're going to start out in the morning."

Al and Lan shrugged, set out of the lean-to, and tended to their pre-slumber business. They unrolled their bedrolls and set their saddles at one end for use as pillows. The twigs on the ground crinkled as the men set up their bedrolls. The scent of pine trees filled their nostrils. Neither had bothered with much of a response to John's rhetorical question about satisfaction.

While they were outside the lean-to and out of John's earshot, Lan asked Al something that he'd been wondering ever since he learned about the Williams brothers. "Where does John gets that black nature of his? You're nothing like him, but you're brothers."

"I know. It's hard to understand." Al paused and related his story. "Our parents were killed when John was just ten years old and I was six. Our family had a little range herd, and we were barely able to feed ourselves.

"Back then, the mountain men took a pretty dim view of settlers. In their view, we were crowding them, and that made them more dangerous than the Indians.

"One night, a few of them came down from a drunken rendezvous in the hills. They raped my mother and killed her and our father. John hid me in a corner of the root cellar and probably saved our lives."

Lan shook his head, "What horror you two must have faced. But I don't see . . ."

"From that time on, John took care of us both," Al continued. "He couldn't make a living with his head, and we were just kids. We had no schooling to speak of, and using our backs never paid well, so he steered us into crime. We left the ranch and got into petty stuff, at first. But John kept dreaming up bigger and riskier jobs. Eventually, his reputation grew to what it is now. I think we've been lucky, but we've survived. I owe John for that."

"But why the insane cruelness? He's an animal."

"Hold it. He's my brother."

"I'm sorry, but he's inhuman."

Al grimaced and then acknowledged the truth of Lan's statement. "When we were first on our own, we didn't do very well. John kept reminding me about how those mountain men came down and did whatever they wanted. They got what they wanted and got away with it. That attitude became John's model for success. We did our first armed robbery when he was eleven, and John killed his first man then. Ever since, ruthlessness has been his trademark and his path to getting what he wants."

"So, a spirit of revenge has turned him into a monster."

"He might be a monster, but he's still my brother."

"You know he's not normal."

"But he's taken care of me all these years. That was no easy task. We were just kids. I have to excuse his bizarre behavior out of thanks. The fear it creates helps keep us alive. What lawman or other outlaw wants to cross paths with John Williams?"

"I guess you're right," Lan said. He pulled his hat down. "I know I'll be better off with you guys than on my own. I just needed to know where you stand and to find out what I could about John's nature. That knowledge may help keep me out of John's gun-sight someday."

Al turned to look at Lan. "You having second thoughts about joining up with us?"

"Naw. It's just scary. I'll never be able to relax. Don't tell me you accept it either. I see you cringe whenever John acts up. And what about that fight you just had?"

Al dropped his gaze to the ground. "Sometimes I can hardly stand being around him."

Lan looked over to where John was preparing to turn in for the night. "What does John want?"

Al's voice softened, indicating he shared at least a portion of this one goal with his brother. "John wants to have a gang that will run the whole territory. To him, that will make up for not being smart enough or good enough at anything to make it in this world without resorting to crime."

Lan couldn't help but wonder how much of that was John's idea and how much was just Al's explanation.

BADMAN, Polzin

From the cover of the rocks at the top of the hideout rim, the three outlaws carefully scanned the landscape surrounding Lander.

"It doesn't look like any law has gotten up this way yet," John said. "It's pretty unlikely that anyone is going to find this little rock arch, and that's the only way they'll ever find the hideout. I doubt there's anybody in town who really wants to find it."

"It looks as if you're right," Lan said. He squinted and scanned the landscape. "I don't see anything out there bigger than a rabbit."

The three men mounted their horses and rode down the gentle slope. They were headed to a place where no one knew them. They had agreed on Red Lodge, Montana. It had all the women John could want and plenty of whiskey. Al and Lan considered it as safe a place for them as any, and the ride there would keep them in the high country, among the trees, and out of sight for most of the distance to their destination.

They traveled slowly, picking their way through and among the rocks, streams, and trees as they wound along the east side of the continental divide. For hours, they forced their horses along the steep hills and fought to stay in their saddles on the rough, jolting trek.

The density of the trees increased as the trip progressed. Occasionally, they saw quick movements, just at the edge of their vision. Sometimes it was a rabbit, sometimes a deer, and sometimes just a tree waving in the wind. With each of these movements, the tension in Al and Lan increased. The fear of encountering a posse searching for them, or any other confrontation, weighed heavily on their minds. But John thrived on apprehension. The flashes of movement added excitement to an otherwise dull ride.

John took advantage of the distractions and killed any of the animals whose movements were too slow to escape his gun. Each gunshot sent terror through Al and Lan, who pictured curious Utes or lawmen converging on them from all sides.

John rode slightly ahead of the others, obviously anxious for a different kind of sport—the kind that Red Lodge offered. Al and Lan rode side by side. Their nearly identical sorrel mounts matched stride for stride along open stretches. The two men did not desire to join ranks with the man in front of them.

On the afternoon of the third day, Lan saw a blur in the trees. "Al, did you see that? I saw something move over there in the trees, about a hundred yards in that direction, maybe a little more." He pointed in the general direction.

"Naw, I didn't see anything," Al said. He tried to sound calm. "It was probably just a bird or something, but we can't afford to be caught off guard."

"What are you boys talking about?" John asked as he whirled his horse around, toward Al and Lan.

Lan controlled his rising ire and turned toward John with quiet, calm words. "I thought I saw something move in the woods over there." He pointed in the general direction. "Twice now. It's probably just an animal."

"Well, let's check it out." John changed direction and sped off across the rugged terrain.

※ ◎

Al and Lan set out after him at a more cautious pace. Then something caught Al's eye. "Wait. John, stop."

Fifty yards out, John's horse pulled up sideways, and John fell awkwardly off the side nearest the others. A shot rang out almost simultaneously.

"Hit the dirt," John yelled. A group of mounted men appeared to be in confused disarray not far beyond him. "Lawmen." John covered his head. "They must have been combing the area. They must have guessed we'd be moving under cover as much as possible and guessed our location."

John's charge obviously had taken the lawmen by surprise, but instant recognition had drawn immediate response. It was a good thing John had realized his blunder, reined in his horse abruptly, and made the unconventional dismount—just in time to save himself from the bullets.

There were four men, the marshal from Lander and his deputies, in the posse. They had safely ensconced themselves behind trees and rocks and were only separated from the outlaws by a twenty-five-yard space.

"Stay down, John," Lan said. "We'll try to draw some of their fire."

Al, still mounted on his horse, charged toward John and dismounted when he got to him. Shots whizzed by as he collected John and they took cover behind their horses.

※ ◎

Lan was next to make the charge, which gave John and Al a chance to climb back onto their horses and get away. When Lan saw that they were clear, he turned around and headed for cover, thankful to still be alive.

Once the Williams Gang found cover, they returned fire. The fact that the lawmen were all clustered together gave the outlaws a small advantage. It was a relatively easy matter for them to put the posse in a crossfire, which denied it retreat or advance.

"Look at them, all close together," John said. "I wish I had some firepower—a Gatling gun or a cannon."

The gunfight raged sporadically for a quarter of an hour, with no casualties. Finally, in an obvious attempt to get a clear shot at the gang, a deputy leaned away from his protective tree. John's shot had just enough room to find its target.

The death of one of their number, accompanied by John's blood-curdling laughter, made the ranchers and shop owners, who had been deputized for the posse, lose their already tentative taste for battle. It had been difficult to get anyone to volunteer to go out looking for John Williams. Now, the two men and even the marshal wanted nothing more than to escape with their lives.

One of the men, a middle-aged storekeeper, rose from his hiding place and grabbed the reins of his horse.

As the man turned his back to the outlaws to mount, John shot him. The other two lawmen got to their horses.

"John, we've got them running," Lan said. "Let them go."

"Where's the fun in that?" John retorted. He turned back toward the fleeing men and fired his pistol again. The remaining posse set their horses off at a fast rate as John fired wildly and cursed Lan.

"Look what you did," John said. "You distracted me long enough to let them get away." John grabbed the reins of his own horse, threw himself into the saddle, and set out in pursuit of the retreating remnant of the posse.

"Let them go," Al said. "Let's get out of here."

"You'll get yourself shot," Lan said.

John ignored their pleas and followed the departing lawmen long enough to get one good shot at their backs. The impact from John's bullet drove one of the men from his saddle to the ground. The marshal rode on without looking back.

John pulled his horse up to the dead man. He fired two more shots into the body. Then he titled his head back in his characteristic, raucous laugh.

After a moment or two, John returned to where his brother and Lan were waiting. "Know who that marshal was?" John asked Lan, smiling. "That was Glen Herman."

"We don't need to tangle with him," Lan said. "Is he the marshal in Lander now?"

"Yep."

"Yeah," Al said, "John's real excited about outdoing the outlaw-turned-lawman."

John scowled at his brother, but only for a second. "Well, what are we waiting around here for? Red Lodge is a ways off yet." John brushed his horse past the other two. "I can hardly wait to meet some of those Montana women. John spurred his mount, making catching up difficult for Al and Lan. But after a few hundred yards, they did pull up beside him. He grinned. "You were right, Al. This trip was a great idea."

Al puzzled over the credit.

"I haven't had so much fun in a long time," John said. "Did you see those cowards run?" He looked at Lan. "You weren't much good, though. Don't you think it's about time you started packing a six-gun?"

Lan just shook his head.

John rode on, continuing to send teasing remarks over his shoulder as he increased the distance between them again.

For a time, the three rode along in silence, with the gap between riders varying. Near dark, the distance was narrowed considerably.

Suddenly, John pulled up on the trail and sighed. "We forgot to clean out the dead men's pockets. Quite a gang I've got. One man don't carry a gun, and the other one don't want to kill anybody. And neither of them thinks to rob the bodies. Maybe I can find a recruit in Red Lodge — somebody who can be some help." John rode away from them again.

The outlaws spent the night camped near a stream in the mountains. After they arranged the bedrolls and started a fire for their coffeepot and beans, the conversation began to flow.

"It's a shame Marcia couldn't come along with us," John said. "But I don't think she'd be much interested in the girls in Red Lodge." He took a bite of beans from his cup. "She'd have had fun, though, I think. Come to think of it, I'm never sure what she likes."

"Lan, how'd you get started as an outlaw?" Al asked.

"I got tired of playing cow's best friend. I grew up on a ranch. I never found the great thrill in a round-up or branding or a cattle drive. It's hard, dirty work. So, one day, I took off on my own. I never saw my parents again.

"My father didn't like guns any better than I do. He'd never let me have one. He said I was too young to need it, and if I didn't need a gun, I shouldn't have one. So, when I left, I had no six-shooter." Lan sipped some coffee and took a bite of beans.

"The first town I hit, I got into a scuffle with a troublemaker." Lan glanced toward John. "I pummeled the bully to the ground. A promoter from a carnival was in town, saw me, and liked what he saw. He took me in and trained me. I started fighting on the circuit, back east a little ways — St. Louis, Leadville, and Jefferson City. I could have stayed at it . . . I never got beat. But the money wasn't good, and even the winner takes a beating. So, I robbed my trainer/manager, trying to get rich quick, and took off. That's pretty much the story.

"From then on, it was one thing or another to get by. The money still wasn't any good, but that's gonna change now." Lan stopped speaking for a minute. He knew the scar under his right eye testified to his hard life. "If I would have had a gun when that first guy picked a fight, I'd probably be dead. That fact made me a permanent believer in being unarmed."

Al nodded with understanding. The outlaws finished tending to the business of eating and cleaning up before they noticed that John had turned in for the night and was curled up in his bedroll, asleep.

"Your story makes me think about a job John and I did a long time ago," Al said. "It was the first time I saw him shoot an unarmed man. He's earned his reputation. But the fear it has put in people has kept us safe up to now."

"Tell me about the shooting," Lan said.

"I really don't want to think about it. What's there to say? He just shot this guy for no reason at all. That's it. It could have been you. If John had been that bully you faced, it would have been you."

Lan shuddered. Being unarmed might not be as safe as he thought.

Al and Lan curled up in their blankets and soon joined John in sleep.

A few days later, the outlaws rode into Red Lodge. The town was bustling, even though it was near evening. The men looked around and saw businesses standing side by side in a stationery parade through the middle of town. The street, which was deeply rutted, was lined with boardwalks. It was early autumn, but none of the occasional early autumn weather that occurs in south central Montana had abated the summer heat.

John searched the main street, eyeing the saloon.

A man in rugged ranch-hand clothing stumbled toward the outlaws, but before he could pass, John's horse blocked his path.

"Where's the nearest saloon?" John asked.

The man was obviously drunk and having a difficult time speaking.

"Come on cowpoke, I haven't got all night."

The man swayed, but he still seemed to sense a need for caution. "Sunshine S-S-S-haloon is right here." He pointed to the sign hanging over his shoulder.

John pushed the man aside, dismounted, then headed for the saloon.

Al and Lan looked around as they dismounted and tied their horses to the hitching rail. They noted the staggering man carefully making his way across the street after his meeting with John.

"Did you notice the jail down the street?" John asked, when the others caught up with him at the saloon door.

"No," Al said.

"I saw it," Lan said. "I didn't pay much attention to it, though. Why?"

"I always get a little sick when I'm near one of those places," John said. "It's all I can do to keep from throwing up. I won't ever be inside of one of those. I'll die first."

Lan nodded. *The fact that the mountain men who killed his parents never had to face justice has something to do with how he feels. And it's hard to blame to him.*

The heels of the outlaws' boots clomped on the boardwalk as they entered the Sunshine Saloon. John paused just inside the doorway and they all looked around. Through the crowd, the green felted tables stood out against the sawdust-covered floor. Kerosene lanterns hung from wagon-wheel chandeliers, and the bar, which covered the back wall, had a backdrop of a mirror covered with a painting of a reclining, nude woman. On the left of the room was a small stage next to stairs that climbed the wall.

"Look at all them women," John said.

The abundance of women John was excited about amounted to a half-dozen bar girls and waitresses. John wasted no time and headed for the nearest one.

Al and Lan glanced around, wondering if they might be walking into trouble. They stepped up to the bar, and each ordered a whiskey.

John grabbed a woman from the lap of a cowboy dressed all in black and wearing a straight-brimmed hat banded at the crown by a row of silver coins.

"And just what do you think you are doing?" the cowboy asked.

"She was the closest woman," John said, as if his reasoning were obvious. He gave no hint of backing down.

The man in black rose from his chair and scraped it backward across the wooden floor. Conversations around the room stopped.

The woman struggled to free herself of John's grasp and stepped aside as John prepared to go for his gun. She suddenly changed her direction and stepped between the two men, placing her hand on John's gun hand. "Hold it, fella," she said with an authority that made it seem highly likely to Lan that she was the owner of the saloon. She turned toward the cowboy. "You too, Bo."

The woman was a little stocky, but she was shapely enough to arouse the cowboys she served. She held her ground between John and Bo.

John relaxed a little but watched his adversary closely over the woman's shoulder.

"You'd better learn some manners if you want to get anywhere with Sally Finch, stranger."

Sally looked back toward Bo. "Sit back down and enjoy your drink. I'll be back later."

Sally looked at the stranger and saw an unwashed man who exuded badness. But she also noted his trim body, self-assurance, and an unidentifiable something that attracted her.

She started to walk past John, and he grabbed her arm, pulling her to him. Bo's tenseness returned, and he squared around, ready to draw his gun. All around the room, Sally noticed anticipatory movements. The noise level remained negligible.

"You better be careful if you want to stay alive around here," she said. She smiled and nodded in the general direction of her protectors. She was in control and planned to go off to tend her business. "It'll be alright, boys," she assured the men in the bar. "The man will behave himself . . . won't you? What's your name?"

John walked her over to Al and Lan before answering. John's two partners were still keeping a watchful eye on the room.

John made introductions. "Sally, this is my little brother, Al. This one is Lan Phelan." Then after a pause, he puffed out his chest. "And I'm

John Williams."

The outlaws looked around the saloon. All three were looking for signs of recognition. Al and Lan feared it. John expected and hoped for it.

There was no reaction. Many of the customers had quietly left. The men, and few women, who had remained through the threat of danger returned to their own business. The previous noise level was nearly restored.

❧ ❧

John tried to order a drink for the lady. "Bartender," John said, "slide two beers down the bar." His disappointment at the lack of response to his name barely showed.

"Let's find a table and sit down," Sally said.

"What's wrong with right here? I like the bar," John said. He held onto Sally's elbow.

She tried to squirm away. "A lady doesn't drink standing up."

"Well, then, let's go to your room." John bounced his eyebrows up and down before grabbing her arm more firmly and starting for the stairs that lined the wall. He assumed her room would be on the second floor.

Instead of resisting, Sally called to the bartender. "Jim, give me a bottle of the good whiskey."

John grabbed the bottle from the bartender's hand as it materialized over the top of the bar.

"Thanks, Jim." John laughed. "Al, Lan, I'll be back in a little bit. Enjoy yourselves. I intend to." He grinned at Sally as the two of them slid across the room.

Sally's expression was an inquisitive smile. It seemed she felt unwilling to stop this strange man's advances.

❧ ❧

Everyone in the saloon watched as Sally and John mounted the stairs. John's two allies kept a wary eye on the others for signs of trouble, but it seemed no one cared much what went on, as long as Sally didn't seem to mind. Everyone seemed convinced Sally knew what she was doing.

The twosome climbed the stairs, and Sally halted John outside the first room. "This is my room," Sally said. She gestured for John to open the door.

As John swung the door open, they crossed the sill together into the dimly lit bedroom. The sole lamp, with its wick down, illuminated the luxurious furnishings. A tapestry couch and canopied bed dominated the room.

"Now, this is what I call style," John said.

He set the bottle on a stand at the end of the sofa and pulled Sally into his arms. She returned his caress fervently, though with more tenderness. Their lips met in an extended kiss, after which John pulled Sally to the bed.

"Whoa, cowboy. You don't waste any time, do you?" Sally struggled free and removed herself to a chair. "How about a drink?"

"Sure," John said. He walked to her side.

Sally uncorked the bottle and found two glasses nearby. They sipped their drinks as Sally made an attempt at small talk. "Where are you from, John Williams?"

John nuzzled her cheek while his free arm wrapped around her waist. "Wyoming."

They set their drinks down, and John sought Sally's lips again. Sally sighed when his hand found its way to her derriere.

Al and Lan found themselves in a poker game, still waiting for John to return from the room upstairs.

Finally, he appeared at the railing above the barroom, Sally on his arm. The couple came slowly down the stairs as the poker players watched their progress. Their steps were careful and leisurely, hinting at tenderness, as well as insobriety and sleeplessness. They joined the men at the poker table.

"I sure hope you boys enjoyed yourselves as much as I did." John grinned widely and glanced at Sally. She was smiling too.

"This partner of yours sure doesn't take 'no' for an answer," Sally told Al and Lan.

"We know what you mean," Lan said.

"To tell you the truth, John, we were bored to death, and a little worried too," Al said. "We thought something might have happened to you."

"Oh, it did. It surely did." John laughed.

Sally joined in the laughter. She patted John's shoulder.

"I ain't felt so good since I don't know when."

"I think we should be looking for a place to spend the night," Lan said.

"Sure, sure," John said. "But I've been in bed enough for a little while."

Sally turned her head away.

"What's your hurry, Lan?"

"We haven't had any sleep for a long time," Al said. "We're going over to that hotel across the street and get a room. Are you coming?"

"Getting mighty pushy, ain't we, Al?" John said. "Now, looky there . . ." John gestured toward a young girl serving drinks to some men at another table. "That one's got all the right stuff in the right places. How's that suit your fancy?"

Sally glared at him.

"That's a right nice little filly," John said.

"Nice is right," Sally said. Her eyes reflected jealousy and protectiveness. "Sheila is just a waitress. That's all . . . understand? Besides, she's just a kid."

The girl, who appeared to be about nineteen, continued her work while John leered at her blue-frocked body.

"Sally, you don't think I was looking at her for me, do you?" John asked with make-believe pain in his voice. "I was just thinking how good a couple Al and her would make. Don't you think so, brother?"

"I . . ." Al stammered.

"You're not interested in this gorgeous—"

Sheila screamed as John reached out and grabbed her chest as she passed close to him. John bent and offered the hem of Sheila's skirt to Al. Sheila screamed again.

"She's not available," Sally shouted above Sheila's screams, trying to wrestle the girl away from John. Sally grabbed John's hand and pulled it free of the girl's clothing.

The two men that Al and Lan had been playing poker with left. The men that Sheila had been serving simply stared in shock. It was obvious that nobody wanted to get involved with this wild man.

John shoved Sally and started after Sheila. Sally landed in a heap on the floor. The rest of the men in the saloon quietly slipped away, avoiding possible trouble.

"Well, if Al doesn't want her, I guess I'll have to make sure she isn't totally neglected after all."

Sally was up and tugging his arm again.

"Sally, you sure are a pain all of a sudden."

Sheila was trying to put distance between herself and John.

"I guess I'll move to greener and less demanding pastures." John caught up with Sheila and grabbed her by the waist with one arm and placed the other under her, picking her up. He tossed her head over his right shoulder and smacked her bottom. "How do you like being a sack of grain? That smack was just for fun. Quit squirming, or I'll let you see how I really have fun."

"John Williams, you put her down," Sally said.

"Well, I can see I'm certainly not going to get to enjoy her company here," John said. He looked around the room and noticed that no one remained except the five of them. "I guess I'll have to take her with me."

Sheila's knee was nudging at John's chin, but it had no effect. Her position kept the blows from having much impact. Her fingers clawed at his back without much better effect. "My father will take care of you," Sheila managed to say between her animal screams.

"John, put her down," Al said. "Let's not cause any trouble."

"Too late, little brother. I'm leaving with the girl. You coming?" John's hand smacked Sheila's behind again and then came to rest on his gun butt.

Lan looked toward Al. "Oh no," was all Lan could say.

"That girl's father is a circuit judge," Sally said. "You're going to be in a heap of trouble, John." Sally followed him to the swinging doors.

Al and Lan crept through the doors, leading John, with Sheila still over his shoulder, kicking and screaming.

Sally broke through the doorway with an angry scream of her own. She darted after John, grabbing at him. John shook her off, throwing her to the ground and off the boardwalk.

⁕

Al was thankful that Bo, the man in black who John first confronted in the saloon, had left. He surely wouldn't have slinked out of sight like the other men.

The girl on John's shoulder was still kicking and screaming when the retreating group reached the horses.

"I'm tired of your fighting, girl," John said. He set her on her feet and slugged her on the chin. She crumbled to the ground, unconscious. "Now, that's more like it. I don't like my women noisy." He laid her across the back of his saddle as if she were a bag of beans.

Sally found her way back to her feet as the Williams Gang mounted their horses. They rode off, leaving Sally standing by the hitching rail, waving her arms and screaming at them.

As the outlaws rode out of town, the way they had entered — past the jail — Al heard people pouring into the street from buildings. The yelling and shouting grew.

"Somebody get the sheriff," said one spectator. "They've got the judge's daughter."

"Don't shoot," someone else said. "You might hit Sheila."

John drew his gun and fired at the first people he saw. One of the men dropped face first into the dirt. The man's gun was still holstered.

Al shook his head.

After what seemed to be an unusually long time, the outlaws cleared the last building in town and veered North, galloping at top speed toward the hills.

No one mounted a horse to give chase. The sheriff had not yet appeared. The crowd's murmuring was accented by Sally's violent screams, and they milled around the dead man as the Williams Gang disappeared.

BADMAN, Polzin

4

The next day, high in the mountains, the temperature was only in the thirties, but all three men had consumed the whiskey John brought along, so they barely even noticed the cold.

"Look at that skin," John said. He beamed as he pulled the tied and conscious girl from his saddle. "Fresh and smooth. What do you bet she's a virgin?"

Sheila's eyes blazed. She had spent the night bound and curled in John's arms, sharing his bedroll. John's molestations had been limited to fondling and kissing the fully clothed girl, until he had drunk himself to sleep. Then, she too had slipped into slumber.

"We've got to get rid of her, John," Lan said.

"I don't know what you're gonna do, Lan, but I'm gonna enjoy her." John bent over to nibble on Sheila's ear.

"John, she's a judge's daughter," Al said.

Sheila nodded threatening agreement.

"We should just leave her here," Al said. "They'll find her. If she's unharmed, maybe they won't be too interested in tracking us down."

John did not respond. Al's words had fired him up even further. Without a word, John picked up the girl and laid her across his shoulder.

He started toward a large landslide of medium-sized boulders. Sheila screamed and squirmed as best she could. Her eyes were wide with terror.

"Have you thought about Marcia?" Al asked. He used the name John would react to, hoping he could redirect John's thoughts.

"Shut up," John said. He winced with pain as Sheila momentarily gained enough movement to head-butt him. "Leave Marcia out of this. Understand?"

Al lowered his head and turned away.

Lan stared at Al. "You can't just let him do it."

John made a movement toward the rocks again and then turned back. His tone of voice changed radically as he addressed his partners. "Say, why don't we take turns with her? What do you say?" John swung the girl, rear first, toward Lan and then Al.

"I don't think so," Al said. He waited for another outburst.

"Still going to pass up a good thing, eh? Well, I'll get her all broke in and warmed up for you, in case you change your minds later."

Sheila's eyes begged Lan for help.

Lan's eyes settled on the girl, but not for long. He couldn't bear to look at her face.

"What was that?" John asked. "Perhaps she's not to your liking. Do you want to go back to Red Lodge and find another one?"

Lan and Al walked away. Their purposeful strides meant to carry them quickly away from the guilt Sheila made them feel for not coming to her rescue. They just wanted to get far away from Red Lodge, without the girl.

"Well, I'll just have to keep her all to myself then."

Al turned back toward his brother again. "We've got to get rid of her." He crouched in the classic gunfighter pose, his hand expectantly near his six-shooter.

"Why? Because she's a judge's daughter?" John laughed. He finally let Al's fears sink in. He looked at the girl. "Little girl, judge's daughters shouldn't do the things we're about to do."

The girl's eyes burned with hatred.

Still laughing, John grabbed the girl's arm and twisted it, delighting in her pained reaction. Then he pushed the girl from his shoulder. She stumbled but kept her balance.

"Al tried once more to reason with John. "We've got to leave her here. When they find her, they'll be too busy taking care of her to worry about us." Al knew his logic wasn't sound, but he hoped John wouldn't notice. None of them had forgotten about the man John killed in Red Lodge. "We can travel faster without her. We can stay out of sight easier, and if we need to, we can fight better without someone resisting us the whole time."

John glared at his brother. "Little brother, you're pushing me again." John spit. "Look at her, would you? Her people ain't gonna just forgive us if we let her go. We've spoiled the judge's little girl. And then there's that dead man."

"But nothing has really happened to the girl yet . . ." John's narrowing eyes stopped Al.

"Something's gonna happen, Al," John said. He began dragging the girl out of sight, behind the boulders. "I like a little privacy."

Al saw that all hope for her was gone.

"If I'm gonna be hanged, I'm gonna make sure I make it worthwhile." John laughed loudly.

Al and Lan could bear the girl's screams only so long, so they wandered away from camp. When they returned, over an hour later, the girl was seated on the ground, near the horses. She was still rope-bound and was gagged again.

Lan and Al tried to persuade John to let Sheila go again. But he refused.

"Let's hold her for ransom." John smiled. "Her old man must have money, or at least friends who do. I figure we've already taken the risk. We might as well make it pay off." John stood up from where he had been seated at the campfire.

Al and Lan stared at one another. Collecting ransom would only add fuel to her protectors' vengeance. Besides, it meant dealing far too closely with the people whose only satisfaction would be in hanging them. There was no way to tell John that. There was no way to change John's mind, but Al felt forced to try something.

"Great idea," Al said.

"What?" Lan whispered.

"But how do we let them know she's being held for ransom?" Al paused, thinking. "We'll need a place to hide her while we deal with her people. Maybe Marcia would allow us to leave her at the ranch." Al searched John's face to see how he would react to his bringing up Marcia's name this time. His idea was to present John with a situation so undesirable that he would abandon the whole ransom idea.

John was silent for a moment, and then he erupted. "Are you nuts? I don't want Marcia involved in this. Forget it. Besides, Sheila can stay with us and keep us warm on these icy nights."

"But she'll make it easier for them to catch us," Al said. He abandoned his reverse psychology as a lost cause.

"We can't just leave her somewhere," John said. He scratched his head. "We've got to have her in order to ransom her. If she wants to stay alive, she won't give us any resistance." John glared at Sheila.

Al weighed the prospects of confronting John further and decided against it.

"She stays with us, and we're going to collect a ransom," John said. "That's that."

Al and Lan wandered away from the fire and out of earshot.

"Who is Marcia?" Lan asked.

"She may be the only person in the world who John really cares about—that includes me. But he has a hard time dealing with that. He believes caring is equal to being weak. That's something he can't tolerate." Al nodded his head in John's direction. "There's a strange chemistry between them. I can't understand what either of them wants with the other one. Marcia wants a man who'll settle down on the ranch with her. That's sure not John. John wants a sexy, adventurous woman. That's not the Marcia I perceive; although, I've never even met her. John always goes to her ranch alone. But she sure sounds like a homebody to me. I thought bringing up her name might get his mind off Sheila, but . . ." He shrugged.

Lan reviewed Al's explanation in his mind as he walked toward John's horse, where John was making preparations to lift the girl onto its back. They were almost ready to leave. Lan helped John lift the girl up behind the saddle.

John started untying the ropes and removed the gag from Sheila's mouth. The ripped and shredded remains of her clothes fluttered in the breezy air. She sat erect, quiet—her tears barely held back.

"You heard what we've said," John said to her.

She closed her eyes and appeared to be saying a prayer.

"I'm turning you loose. You just head back the way we came and find your papa. You tell him not to come after us. We wouldn't be bashful about killing a few more lawmen. Now, get out of here."

John swatted the horse's rump with his hand. The horse bucked and broke into a run. Sheila guided the horse through the clearing and disappeared among the trees.

John whipped around to face his partners. "Well, what do we do now?"

Incredulous, Al said what seemed to be the only thing that came to his mind. "Are we heading back to the hideout?"

"What about our trip?" John asked. His gleaming eyes said the recent events were already forgotten. He was looking forward to more excitement.

"John," Lan offered with enthusiasm and excitement, hoping to sweep John along, "I'm anxious to get back to the hideout."

"Already tired of running all around the countryside? Yeah, me too." There seemed to be something else on John's mind.

Lan mounted his horse with a silent sigh of relief and waited while Al swung into the saddle behind John. Lan's horse carried most of their gear, making a heavy load for both horses.

Slowly, with mixed feelings among the men, they headed back to Wyoming. But the thoughtful silence was broken by John only a few yards along the trail as snow started to fall. "You're right, Lan. It's time to get back to work." John laughed.

It chilled Lan's blood.

The Williams Gang wound their way along the continental divide as they headed back to their hideout. They picked their way along the same tree and rock-cluttered mountains they had traveled on their way to Red Lodge, avoiding the most direct route for fear of running across more posse activity and to make pursuit from Red Lodge more difficult. Having two heavily laden horses made it impossible to cover ground rapidly.

Soon snow began to accumulate, making passage even more difficult. John noted the increasing crispness in the air. The temperature was dropping. It would be a cold night, especially as they climbed even higher into the mountains. The leaves on the deciduous trees were multicolored, and the days were growing shorter. Yet, all the depressing things about fall only added excitement and animation to John's disposition.

For their part, Al and Lan found the monotonous crossing of the streams and the climbing and descending of the tedious inclines an irritation. On occasion, they thought they smelled burning wood. Whether it was campfires, forest fires, or the remnants of an Indian raid on a ranch, they could not tell.

Two years of a peace treaty with the Sioux had been a joke. Red Cloud had persuaded the cavalry to abandon Fort Kearny in return for a guarantee of no interference with the Union Pacific rail line in their territory. Unfortunately, Governor Campbell could do little to control the actions of the ranchers that formed the majority of the white population. They were not known for giving the Sioux and Cheyenne a fair break. As a result, the treaty was pretty much one-sided in its adherence. What's more, the Utes didn't consider the treaty binding on them at all, and rumblings of gold in the Black Hills were causing more nervous reactions among both white and red men.

The weather was undeniably cold by the time the Williams Gang was a day from home, causing the moisture from their breath to freeze on their mustaches. They were high in the Rockies, and snow fell heavily.

John's mood changed. "What's wrong?" he quietly asked the horse Al and he were riding. "You don't like the cold?"

"Hey, Al," John said to Al. "This horse is cold. You got another blanket?"

Al didn't respond, but he was curious. John rarely cared about the horse he was riding. Al glanced at Lan. His look said that John's pensive mood puzzled him too.

That night, they were concerned about their fire being spotted and causing them trouble, but it was too cold to do without one. So far, they'd been lucky. After they settled in, they saw another fire in the distance. Following that discovery, they rose early to avoid crossing paths with the other travelers; although, John suddenly expressed a desire for some break in the monotony. He preferred and a confrontation to "sneaking around like a coward." But once they were on the move again, John's mind sprinted off in another direction.

"You guys go on ahead to the hideout without me," John said. "I'll show up later. I've got something I want to take care of."

Lan knew that if John left, he would be taking one of the horses, thus forcing Lan to share the remaining horse with Al the rest of the way, perhaps loaded with their goods as well as two men. Yet, Al seemed relieved. Lan wondered if Al had considered what kind of trouble John could get into on his own. The thought of new trouble frightened Lan, but Al's peace of mind meant he knew something.

They halted the horses and, without much talk, started dividing their belongings, combining Al's and Lan's things onto one horse.

"I don't need all my stuff," John said. "You can take the bedroll with you and some of these other things."

The horse John was loading began to walk off. "Stand still," John said.

Immediately after the outburst, a modest one for John, he looked up at the other two men. His expression softened. "Excuse me," he whispered.

Lan shook his head in disbelief.

John turned his attention back to the horse, which kept increasing its distance from the men and the other horse.

Lan took advantage of the increased distance to lean close to Al and ask quietly, "What's going on?"

"Does John's gentleness puzzle you?" Al chuckled.

"It scares me," Lan said. "Sorry, I know he's your brother, but it's obvious John is not normal; and when he acts normal, it makes me think he is up to something."

"Marcia lives just east of here," Al said. "That's where he's going. He's been thinking about her. He won't say so, of course. He won't let me go there with him, let alone you, so he made an excuse to go off alone. He always gets quiet and calm when he's thinking about going to see her. She's special to him. She's always giving him a hard time about settling down and rounding off his rough edges, but he puts up with it. They fight, he fumes, and after a day or two of it, he's back at the hideout all wound up again and ready to shoot somebody for the fun of it. But he keeps going back. I guess he unconsciously starts practicing manners before he gets to her place." He chuckled again.

"I'm not sure what goes on there," Al continued. "He says she's pretty, but he gets all the pretty women he wants, one way or the other. That can't be what makes her special. He's no prize, of course. What she sees in him, I don't know." He kicked a rock and watched it leave a trail in the dirt. "Maybe she's his self-punishment, his penance for being the way he is and living the way he does. But what he means to her . . . I don't understand, unless it's just the challenge, the conquest of controlling a badman. Maybe she uses her femininity or whatever to try to reform him."

Al grinned in the direction of his big brother, who was still struggling with the horse. "Don't let him know you noticed his nice streak, or you'll regret it."

Lan chuckled at the new image of John. "Well, I sure am not thrilled about spending the next few hours on the same horse as you, but I guess if that'll keep John out of trouble for a while, I'm for it." Lan's smile grew.

"The only problem, Lan, is that when he gets tired of Marcia's attempts to reform him, he'll show up back at the hideout more ready to get into trouble than ever."

Lan shrugged. "Well, after all, we are outlaws." He looked up and saw that John had finally succeeded, without any more cursing, to get the horse ready.

"I'll see you guys in a few days," John said as he headed east. "Take care of things. If you two get tired of sharing a horse, there are some ranches around here where you could find another one." He was now a shadow that faintly resembled the outlaw leader of the Williams Gang.

Al and Lan climbed onto their mount and soon left the Owl Creek Mountains behind them. Then in the shadow of the Wind River Range, they entered the Shoshone Basin. They were almost home.

John wound his horse through the trees and rocks of the hills leading down from the Wind River Range. His face wore a light smile, and occasionally, he broke into whistling a tune he had picked up somewhere. At one point during his ride, a rather large lizard skittered across his path, causing John's horse to rear. The man who would normally have killed the lizard and cursed his horse only laughed an entertained laugh.

John, could he have seen himself, wouldn't have believed the sight. It bothered him enough just to feel different; he wasn't hungering for violence. But to see himself smiling kindly and whistling would have been too much for him. Still, in spite of himself, he liked the way he was feeling.

John rounded a large rock outcropping and stopped humming as he gazed far in the distance, where there was a small ranch house. Some lazy blue smoke drifted from the chimney.

He brought his horse to a halt once he had a good view of the house. His disposition softened even more as he remembered the last time he was there. *Maybe I've been a little rough on her. She never raises her voice, and she is more than nice to me—and all of this in spite of her dislike for my way of life.* After a few minutes of contemplation, he let out a quiet, "Hmmph," and continued along the trail.

"If only she wouldn't nag," he said aloud, perhaps to his horse. "How can she expect me to be a rancher?" He nudged the horse's flanks and caused it to pick up the pace. Then, for no apparent reason, John threw his head back, closed his eyes, and let out a deep belly laugh. The horse started and then settled back to a steady walk. The hardened, compassionless outlaw had surfaced for a moment. Thus, that persona was exorcised for the duration of his visit with Marcia.

For a short while, the ranch house was lost to John's view behind a strand of trees. Then the trees cleared, and the house was close at hand.

He saw something move on the porch. It was Marcia, brown-haired and slender, waiting to meet him. It seemed she always knew when he was coming. John didn't know how, but it made him feel special. He liked that feeling, even though he really didn't care about Marcia's feelings.

※◎ ◎※

The truth was that Marcia met all riders when they arrived. She kept a wary vigil, watching the ridgeline. Since there was unrest with the Indians over the treaty breaches, her living alone, in seclusion, had become dangerous.

※◎ ◎※

Marcia evoked a strange feeling in John, but he couldn't deny he enjoyed it. He observed her hair, which was tied efficiently at the back of her head, as always; her well-proportioned chest; and her plain cotton dress, aged and faded. No matter how she was dressed, she looked beautiful to him. He would never concede that, though. But he believed she would look beautiful to anyone, and perhaps he was right.

"Hi, John. It's great to see you."

John dismounted and stepped onto the low porch in two movements. He took Marcia into his arms and swung her side to side. "It's good to see you too," he said quietly. His smile was not his usual one, and his gentleness was a foreign trait to the bad man who had raped Sheila.

"Come on inside," Marcia said. She gestured toward the door. "You've been gone too long."

John released her from his embrace and followed her inside to the combination kitchen, dining, and living room. In this small ranch house, only the bedroom was separated from the rest of the house. John looked around. Blue curtains still covered the costly glass window over the kitchen counter. The main window to the side of the fireplace was only an opening covered by wooden shutters, but it also sported curtains.

They embraced again before they found chairs close to each other.

Marcia began questioning John. "Where have you been all this time?"

"What have you been doing, Marcia?" John countered. He got up from his chair and walked in a small circle before realizing the futility of trying to avoid her question.

She stared at him, waiting for a reply.

He made one more attempt to change the subject as he sat back down. "Why do you live out here all by yourself? The Indians are upset enough with the way the ranchers treat them. Now, there's rumors of gold in the Black Hills. There'll be massacres right and left if there's a gold rush through here."

"I can take care of myself, John Williams." She returned to the original topic. "You've been up to no good again, haven't you? I know that little laugh. Don't try to hide it. You might as well tell me, even though I don't want to hear it."

"Well . . ." John said.

"Oh, John, why can't you just settle down here with me? Then I wouldn't be out here all alone. You love me, don't you? Why won't you marry me?" She paused, searching John's face. After a moment, she answered her own question. "You don't love me, do you? You don't want to marry me." She paused again, waiting for his response.

Her stare made John more uncomfortable than he wished to let anyone make him. "Of course I do, Marcia," he said. "You know that. It's just that . . ." The visit was not going to be a good one. His manner fell to one of moroseness.

~⊚ ⊚~

"You love excitement." She picked up where he left off. She hated to admit it, but his love of excitement was an aspect of him that had drawn her to him and perhaps still held her. When they first met, she didn't know he was an outlaw, but she was overpowered by his ruthlessness. She hadn't seen any other side of him until much later.

She sighed. "I've heard this so many times before. It makes me sick. You can't settle down—you're too restless. I know, you've already told me that." She took her turn at rising and pacing. "I don't know why I put up with it." She stood with her back to him, and after a second, she said, almost too quietly for him to hear, "I guess I do . . . I love you." She wrung her hands and her eyes darted around the room as she waited for him to say something.

Marcia had been married once. They had started the ranch. Then her husband took sick and died. She'd long forgotten the pain and had spent years working the place alone, never growing into a big rancher as she and her husband had dreamed. But with help from friends, she managed to survive.

John said nothing. He just sat in his chair. Marcia knew he'd heard this argument before.

Another moment of silence went by, and then Marcia spoke again. Her mind fought the unwinnable battle, and her heart took charge. John was here, and he was hers for a while. When she spoke, she was under control. "Why don't you unpack your things?" She was about to say, ". . . and stay a while," but she thought better of it.

She walked to the wood-burning range and moved the teakettle to the front to heat water. The money her husband had brought from the East had given them many things others in Wyoming didn't have. She was grateful for not having to cook in the fireplace.

~⊚ ⊚~

"Yeah, I'll unpack . . . but I'm not staying for long." He realized anger tinged his words and softened the impact with covering prattle. "I mean, I have to get back to the boys."

It was obvious his explanation did little to convince Marcia he wasn't referring to what really bothered him at the ranch.

"The boys? You mean Al?" she asked.

There was more silence in the ranch house. Then John said, "I'll stay, but just for a little while."

"Of course."

They turned away from each other. John headed for his horse to unpack, and Marcia headed for the back room to prepare her bed for him. She figured that sleeping with him might be the only thing she could do that would mean enough to him to make him give up his reckless lifestyle to stay with her. Perhaps, with sex, she could exercise a little control over him. He had only been coming to the ranch for a little more than two years, but as yet, he had never forced the issue. She controlled that aspect of their relationship. It was uncharacteristic of his bold ways and uncharacteristic of what had attracted her to him, but she prayed the status would continue.

In the morning, John awoke to the smell of pancakes and eggs. Marcia had a few chickens of her own, but she bought the flour and other essentials in Lander. As John entered the main room, he found Marcia just placing strips of bacon in the iron skillet. Her dress was faded and blue, like the one she had worn the day before, and her apron was a match for his blue denim pants. John gazed at her fresh face and beautiful smile.

"I timed it just right, didn't I?" Marcia said. "I'm starting the bacon now. Sometimes, I think I should get some pigs of my own, but I could never slaughter them myself, so I might as well buy my pork in town."

"Yeah, I think it was the smell of the food that woke me." His tone of voice illustrated that a good night's sleep and the accompanying bedtime activity had helped to smooth away the previous day's irritation.

It dawned on John that they were engaged in small talk. Thus, the conversation over breakfast was easy, and the subject of the future never came up.

"I'll be going to town to vote in a few days. I'm so excited. It's hard to believe I'm one of the few women in the country who is allowed to vote."

"I can't believe any of you are allowed to vote," John said. "What is this world coming to?"

When the dishes were cleared, John helped draw the water for washing them. He always picked around the house, lending aid where Marcia needed it.

Marcia used the luxury of her range to heat the water. When it was hot, John went outside to work on building up the woodpile. It would be a long winter, and the more he did now, the less Marcia would have to do on her own. The air was cool, and it wouldn't be long before it snowed at the ranch. He took an axe and a saw from the pegs on the side of the house, under the porch roof, and threw them into a wheelbarrow Marcia's husband had made. Then he set off for the nearby woods. He was grateful for a chance to vent some of his restlessness in physical activity.

John knew he could never control his violent nature, nor did he want to. He couldn't stand around puttering in the house on a permanent basis—at least, not until he was over sixty. Then maybe he could settle down.

Around noon, John returned with his tenth loaded wheelbarrow and was still feeling restless and hemmed in when Marcia called him for lunch.

"Let's pack this food up and ride off into the woods a ways," John said. "That stream by the base of the hills would be a nice spot to spend some time. We could stay there a while and still get back before dark."

"But there's so much work to be done. Winter's coming, you know. It's not all that warm out today."

"I won't be here forever," he said and immediately regretted it.

Marcia's face fell, and John tried to bring back her smile. "If you don't come with me, I'll go alone." He headed for the door.

Her smile didn't return. The dreaded future had crashed into her consciousness. "Will you come back?" she asked.

"Look, if we've got to talk like this, why not do it out there? You know I can't spend too much time cooped up inside."

The hope that a picnic might help her forget the things she was thinking about made Marcia give in, and they rode into the woods and ate by the stream.

Marcia was bundled in a heavy coat to counteract the nippy fall wind. John settled for his leather jacket and shivered as they sat and talked. She steered the conversation to the status of their relationship.

At first, John tried to match her light, amusing approach to the subject, but once it became obvious that she wasn't going to let it go, he figured he might as well get it over with.

"If you stayed here, the chores wouldn't pile up so high," she explained. "We'd have more time for each other, so we could do this sort of thing. My life would be easier, safer, and less lonely. Doesn't that matter to you?"

"Yeah, of course it does." He knew his look didn't say the same thing. "Sure, I could take you down here by the stream every day during the summer, but you and I both know that wouldn't happen. We would always have more work to do. We would have to get cattle and work to feed them all winter. Then we would have to do the branding and cattle drives. On and on it would go."

"We don't have to do that at all." She tucked a strand of hair behind her ear. "We could stay small."

"Without a lot of work to keep me busy . . . naw, don't go painting me a picture of bliss. I know better."

"John, it wouldn't be like that," she said. "We could grow something so you wouldn't have to worry about cattle. Wouldn't that be better? How about sheep? We could raise sheep. Would that be better?"

"Sheep? You've got to be crazy. You know this territory is run by the cattlemen. They'd skin us alive." He walked off and then turned back to her. He noticed she wasn't following. "We would have to do something to survive. Whatever it was, it would be work. Don't you see? I'm not a working man. I couldn't be tied to a life that made me work when I didn't want to work."

"You outlaw!" she screamed.

"What?" He put his hands up in the air in disbelief. It was always like this when they were together. But it usually took longer to get that way. She had never been so persistent. She didn't seem to be able to talk about anything else. Desperation seemed to be forcing her to make a decision — to decide her direction for the rest of her life right then. Had she finally reached her breaking point after holding on to an impossible dream?

They packed the picnic lunch and rode silently back to the ranch house.

<hr />

Three days into his visit, John decided he'd had enough. He collected his things and started packing his horse. He'd decided that Marcia and what she offered weren't worth the rest of the packaged deal.

<hr />

When Marcia realized he was packing his belongings, she ran from her bedroom doorway to grab his arms. "Don't leave already." She knew it was already settled, and tears flowed from her eyes. She followed him onto the porch in the early morning air and watched him continue his preparations. He didn't bother to speak to her.

For a time, she watched in silence. Then finally, as he cinched his saddle, she could hold back no more. "You thought you could do whatever you wanted here, didn't you? You thought you could just keep coming around whenever you wanted to take me to bed . . . when you wanted a few good meals . . . and then you could leave whenever you wanted. You thought you could do that forever, didn't you? You didn't think you owed me anything, did you?"

<hr />

John wondered why he had loved this girl. Maybe he had just fooled himself. He knew this ranch house was no place for him. He belonged back at the hideout with his gang, planning some new excitement. Whatever it was he had felt for Marcia, he was sure he had outgrown it. "Yeah, well, I've got to get back to my . . . uh, pals."

His gang, that's what he really wanted—not just a kid brother who didn't like killing and another guy who didn't even carry a gun. John wanted a real gang, one that was feared all over the West, one that he could lead ruthlessly, knowing the men would follow his commands unquestioningly. He was sure that if there was enough glory, he could find men who would join.

"Well, I don't care where you go, Mr. Williams. You can't come here whenever you like and leave whenever you like anymore. You can't have no concern for my feelings."

John knew leaving Marcia behind was part of getting his dream to come true. He would probably have to leave Wyoming to gather his gang. It was best that she become part of the past. He would make a fresh start. No more Marcia, no more Wyoming. He hated to leave his perfect hideout behind, but it would be nice to try a new locale, where no one knew him.

There was nothing to hold him there anymore, of that he was sure. He looked at Marcia once more. She was staring at him with her arms crossed in front of her. She said nothing as John stepped back from his horse and mounted the step. He reached out to give Marcia a good-bye kiss.

She drew away from him. "If you think I'm going to kiss you, you're dead wrong. Just get out of here."

Tears fell from Marcia's eyes, but John noticed a resolve in them he had not seen previously.

"Sure, Hon, see you next time." He chuckled in his inimitable way. The chuckle broke into the laugh that she and others knew and hated. He grabbed her roughly, kissed her hard, and pushed her away. Then he stepped back to his horse. "John Williams gets what he wants. Remember that."

In one motion, John was on his way. He never looked back. He didn't see Marcia feebly wave her handkerchief in spite of herself and then use it to dab her eyes until he disappeared from sight.

⚡

While John picked his way among the trees and boulders on the way to the hideout, he planned out the future of his gang. He followed a creek he knew led to the crest of the Owl Creek Mountains. There was a lake there. It was early, and stopping at the lake for a meal of things he'd packed at the ranch would still leave him enough time to make it back to Al and Lan before dark, even through the snow, if he hurried.

John knew his partners wouldn't like his plans, but they would go along. They had to. After all, he was their leader.

John's explanation of his plans for the gang bubbled out of him like water over rocks. "You see, if we head for Tombstone, or somewhere in the Southwest, nobody will know us, and we'll have a run at anything we want. We could have some real fun. All the gangs that are known in the area will draw the law away from us. They might even get the blame for some of the stuff we do." John paused for a moment. "That'll sure keep the law guessing. We could have a real gang. We could get a couple more guys to join up with us. Then we could start taking credit for our own work."

Lan stared at Al, and they both shrugged. It would be nice to leave the dangers of Wyoming for the relative safety of anonymity in Arizona, but with John's tendencies, it wouldn't last very long.

Al knew John's dream well. The most appealing part of the plan for John was the idea that he might be able to recruit more members and form a larger gang, with more notoriety for him.

Al pondered his options. He could go along with the idea, or he could try to persuade John to stay in Wyoming. Even if he succeeded in the persuasion, as unlikely as that was, they would still have to face the local dangers. More importantly, Al realized he could die trying to change his brother's mind. John had been even more irritable than usual since his return from Marcia's ranch.

Then there was another possibility. Al could let John go on by himself. But Al had never been separated from John for any extended length of time since their parents died. Not only did the prospect of finding his own direction not appeal to Al, it had never had been something he considered. It was also possible that mutiny would cost him his life. Leaving John against his will left that possibility wide open.

"OK," Al said. "We'll go to Arizona."

Lan nodded agreement.

"But let's take it easy for a while."

"Ha, ha," John said. "You sure are funny at times, little brother."

The decision was made, so the men began breaking camp. Lan's thoughts concentrated on the dubious intelligence of leaving their safe hideout. *It is only a matter of time before John demands action anyway, and Wyoming is definitely not the safest place for us.* Lan rolled his blankets into a tight cylinder and strapped them behind his saddle. There really wasn't much for him around Lander. He didn't have a Marcia or anything he was particularly fond of, so the move was decidedly a good one for him.

They gathered all of their belongings and were ready for the exodus. They mounted their horses and headed southwest. The plan was to cross the Rockies via South Pass because that was the only route halfway passable at that time of year. They were in no hurry and were prepared with enough essentials to last them if it took a while to cross the mountains. A blizzard could stop their progress for days. They would have to find a cozy place to wait out the storm and then proceed when the skies cleared. It didn't matter. Al and Lan knew no possible hardship could make John put off the trip until spring. And they weren't anxious to convince him to wait, since they feared what mischief John would get them into if they stayed near Lander.

The outlaws spent the whole winter on the Eastern Slope, surviving on the contents of their saddlebags and the game the land offered. Al and Lan did their best to delay their progress. John allowed time to pass, apparently not too intent upon reaching their destination either.

When spring came, the outlaws crossed the Continental Divide and headed south. They met no one on the trail. The only people they saw were in the small towns along the way, where they stopped. They spent the illicit money they had with them. It bothered John to buy anything when it could be stolen, but anonymity was what they were striving for along the way. John didn't want to leave a trail, and they did have to replenish supplies.

On occasion, they spent the night indoors, enjoying a real bed. They usually chose to mingle with townsfolk only after dark, just before the businesses closed. They planned their stays in towns to coincide with snowy nights as much as possible. It gave them comfort when they most needed it and cost them no travel time since they would not be able to make much ground under those conditions anyway.

Each town afforded temptation for John, of course. And eventually, not long after they left Colorado, John could no longer control himself. At the saloon where they were resting, the leader of the gang asserted himself.

"Look, you guys," John said. "I'm going to rob a stage, and you're going to help out. I'm tired of this mamby-pambying around, paying for things."

Lan and Al could only stand and wait for John to go on with his plan.

"Remember that little town in Wyoming, where we stayed the first time we got snowed in? The place where you stopped me from taking that dance hall girl up to my room? Just a few days later, a stage coach came into town with a heavy strong box and just a driver to guard it. A couple of men met the stage, but that only made three of them then. Who knows what was in that box? The way the driver struggled with it, there must have been something heavy in it." The effect of John's first dose of whiskey in days was obvious. "You guys kept saying not to get ourselves in trouble. 'Don't leave a trail,' you said. Like a fool, I listened to you." John swigged another gulp of whiskey.

"There couldn't have been anything valuable in that strong box, or they would have guarded it better," Al said. He ran his forefinger around the rim of his shot glass.

"I'm pretty fed up with both of you, and I've had just about enough of this booze to do something about it." John first looked Al straight in the face and then Lan. "All winter long, you two have had your way. Well, it's just about spring now, and we're not in Wyoming. I'm telling you what we're going to do.

"I saw a stage come into town earlier tonight. This one's not going unmolested. There wasn't any heavy load, and I haven't heard anything about a payroll, bullion shipments, or anything like that, but there were passengers on that stage. Passengers have money, watches, and other valuables. I'm tired of eating rabbit and beans." He slammed his fist against the rough-sawn wall that they were leaning against. "We're running out of money, and my old back needs a real bed more often. So we're going to hit the next stage coach."

Lan peeled a sliver of wood from the wall and began to chew it. Al tugged at his hat brim. They both knew there was no turning John back.

Their leader paced over to the saloon's window and looked out at the dark street. "While you two were lying around in here, I checked the schedule," John said over his shoulder. "There's a stage due here tomorrow morning, early."

Al wasn't thinking about the stagecoach. He was wondering what had happened to their quiet safety. But they were stuck with John's plan.

Lan took the sliver of wood out of his mouth and threw it on the floor. "OK, when do we hit the stage and where?"

Lan answered Al's surprised look with a shrug.

"Well, that's more like it," John said. "I'm glad you're showing a little interest."

"You're right," Lan said, nodding. "We're nearly out of money, and we are outlaws. This is how I expected to earn my living when I signed up."

"There's a flat space, a little draw, southeast of here," John said. "The stage runs through there. I heard some guys talking about all the trouble it has making it through because of the mud from the mountain run off and the rain. We may not even have to stop the stage, it may already be stopped by the mud." John laughed.

"Yeah, our horses will be able to make it through the slosh alright," Lan assured Al. "If there's no gold shipment or anything, there won't be any guards. We might be able to pull it off pretty easily."

Al nodded, but he wasn't happy with the prospects. "Alright, John, you've got your stage holdup, but no unnecessary shooting."

"I say what we do," John retorted. "Now, let's head out to the flats. We'll camp out there tonight."

The stage was moving at a good speed as the three outlaws sprang their horses into action. But soon the big wheels began to get bogged down in the muddy road. It didn't take long for the riders to bring their horses splashing alongside the coach and then stop it. The passengers froze at the sight of John standing there with his gun drawn.

"Alright, everybody put your valuables into this bag as it comes to you," John instructed the passengers.

A portly man, dressed in eastern togs, was the closest to the door. He dropped his pocket watch into the bag. His cuff links and the money from his wallet followed.

He passed the bag to a middle-aged lady next to him. She added her hatpin, necklace, and bracelets to the bag, identifying her valuables and relieving herself of them without further coercion.

The man to her left was less willing to part with his belongings. He dropped his money from his wallet into the carpetbag, and then he handed it across to another young man on the opposite seat.

"Wait a minute," John said. "What about your watch?" he waved his gun. The man removed the watch and dropped it into the bag.

The young man across from him had already started filling the bag with his things.

Next, an attractive young lady in the middle, between the young man and another middle-aged lady, who bore a resemblance to her, dropped her earrings and necklace into the bag without a word.

Finally, the woman closest to the door dropped her jewelry and some money from her purse into the bag. The bag was filled to overflowing by the time all six passengers had given up their personal items.

"You there," John said, pointed at the Easterner. "You, with the fancy suit. You sure you didn't forget anything? Let me see your pockets . . . inside out."

"John, there's no room in the bag anyway," Al said. "We've got plenty. Let's get out of here." He chewed on his bottom lip.

"Maybe this gentleman would be worth a nice ransom," John pointed his gun in the man's direction. "He doesn't have to fit in the bag."

John moved to the middle-aged woman, who still held the bag, and grabbed it. He surrendered the idea of kidnapping the man, figuring he might be more trouble than he was worth. "Count your blessings, mister," John said to the well-dressed man. Then the outlaw struck him hard with the butt of his revolver and laughed as the man sank to the floor of the coach.

Lan and Al, with his gun drawn, had stayed on their horses. John jumped into his saddle, and the three men rode off wildly. John gave a loud whoop.

⚜

The outlaws rode southward. At the next town, they spent the night in real beds and filled their stomachs with good food and drink.

The town was like so many others. They had walked down the main street; hitched their horses in front of the hotel/saloon; and then stomped across the boardwalk, through the swinging doors, and into a noisy room filled with men and a few women.

The Williams Gang went to the bar and ordered drinks. While being served, Al and Lan inquired about where they could get a good meal.

The bartender pointed them to a café up the street, and Al and Lan went for dinner.

John didn't join them. He spent his time gambling, and then he succeeded in talking a lady into spending some time in the room he'd rented for the night. He figured his partners were fine on their own.

As soon as he got the woman in the room, John grabbed her. "Genevieve, that's French, ain't it?" John queried his mistress of the night.

"Oui," Genevieve said.

"Well, that's enough talk," John said. He began to undress her.

"Please, monsieur . . . the light."

"The light stays on. I want to see what I'm getting." He stopped Genevieve from reaching the kerosene lamp on the table.

She surrendered to John. He was pleased to see that the woman had resigned herself to defeat. His fingers quivered as he unbuttoned her bodice.

Al and Lan weren't happy with John for leaving them without any money for the evening. They'd all been a part of the holdup, but John always carried most of the money. With not many options, Al and Lan returned to the saloon. The bartender told them where John was, and the two outlaws decided to retire. They were grateful that John had not caused a ruckus that evening.

The next morning, the gang hit the trail again. Then for weeks, they wandered aimlessly through the late spring rains. The men were able to sleep indoors almost every night, thanks to the take from the robbery. They ate well and stayed in the wilderness only when they mistimed their travel and could not reach a town before darkness fell. Sometimes there was a town only a short distance away, but they didn't know that and gave up before they made the discovery.

For a time, they had no sense of urgency in their travels, and spring eventually slipped into summer. They still had not put much distance between themselves and the location of the stage robbery.

Suddenly, John felt the need to move on, purposefully. "Look, you guys, we've been behaving ourselves for some time now, and the money is running low again. It's hard to spend watches and jewelry. We're back to eating off the land, and it's been a week since I slept in a bed. It's time we got on down to Tombstone."

Al and Lan knew the time would come. It was true, they were out of money. Selling jewelry wasn't easy. They couldn't steal everything they needed forever. Crime was the only income they had. So, they had no choice but to move on to Tombstone.

Al looked at Lan. He knew Lan didn't mind a life of crime. After all, he'd joined the gang permanently in hopes of improving his lifestyle. Wandering in the wilderness was not what he had in mind.

Al, on the other hand, couldn't deny that he enjoyed the feeling of power he got when people cowered before them, but he didn't like the danger of being an outlaw. He was a little ashamed of his lifestyle. He lived with that shame because he believed his place was with his brother. They'd always been together, and he had nowhere else to go. At the same time, Al would have been much happier if he and John were living on the ranch with Marcia. It would have been a new life and, he suspected, a better one.

Unknown to Al or Lan, Marcia was also on John's mind. It was the thought of Marcia that prompted John to suddenly push on to Arizona. He didn't want to be within mind-changing distance if his desire for her increased. It was time to forget Marcia, time to do something about his dream.

Even with John's desire to get to Arizona renewed, it took the trio until early September to get there. The outlaws never seemed to be on a straight line to their destination.

"Once we find civilization again, we're going to knock off a bank," John said. His horse neighed. "I can't stand rabbit stew and beans much longer. I can take the rocks poking me in the back all night. I can sleep through the coyotes howling. But when we find a town, we're hitting the bank and moving on fast. Understand? We'll find another town and spend the night in luxury."

"At least we haven't got a big posse tracking us," Lan said. "We haven't made enough noise for that yet."

⚜

A few days later, they came to a town and hit the bank. The robbery went off without a hitch, and they moved on.

As they rose each morning, Al and Lan would take their time eating. They used as much time preparing their horses for the day's ride as possible, hoping to delay John's appetite for mischief.

Al's thoughts kept turning to Marcia. She represented the only chance to escape the outlaw lifestyle.

⚜

During the latter part of their trip to Arizona, John decided to hit another bank. "This is going to be just like that last bank we did. You go in the back door, Al. I'll go in the front. Lan, since you don't have a gun, you stay outside and warn us if there is any outside interference coming."

They rode into the little town, much like many they had passed through, and split in front of the bank. Al headed around the back. John waited a minute or two and then entered the front door with his gun drawn.

"Everyone against that wall," John ordered, motioning with his gun.

The bank patrons complied, and John handed a bag to a teller.

Another teller behind the cashier's cage turned toward the back door, and Al simply said, "Uh, uh." The man obviously hadn't noticed him standing there with his gun covering the room. The gun-waving John had riveted his attention. The cashier stopped without questioning.

John exited through the front door with the money, while Al covered the escape, backing out the door. Lan had their horses ready, and they fled swiftly.

Before the gang made it past the front of the bank, pursuit flowed from inside. The pursuit died out quickly, though. No one was eager to risk his life to stop the robbers. Thus, a few miles down the trail, the gang slackened their pace and rode on, side by side.

"Well, that certainly didn't go just like we planned. We didn't expect pursuit," Lan said. "Maybe we need to think a little deeper before we take action."

But John's mind was already consumed with planning. What corners of his mind were not filled with plotting filled with anger at his partners for their less than enthusiastic acceptance of the ideas he expressed. He had ideas forming in his mind that would take them into the next two years.

Lan spent his time along the trail trying to figure out how to make his life resemble the one he envisioned when he joined the Williams brothers. He wanted to enjoy the spoils of the outlaw life and spend less time exposed to danger. He sought adventure but not death. John seems to crave both—as long as he was not the one taking the bullet. Lan understood now why John was hated by other outlaws and the law.

It was spring again by the time the Williams Gang stopped wandering around northern Arizona and arrived in Tombstone. They were pleased that the frigid nights had finally given way to hot, bright days, but the gang was out of money, partly because Al and Lan had succeeded in averting many dangerous escapades.

The first thing that caught John's eye as they entered Tombstone was the bank. "Looky there, boys," he said as they neared the town. Then he set his horse off at a full gallop, straight for the bank. "Yahoo!" he yelled as people on the street scattered before his horse.

Al and Lan bolted after John. There was no way to stop him, but they would be near in case he needed help. And it was likely that he would need help. John's exuberance was his worst enemy.

"John, the marshal's office is right next to the bank," Al hollered.

John looked up at the sign on the building next to the bank but did not rein in his horse until he reached the hitching post at the bank. He leaped off his horse, gun drawn, and was on his way into the building before Al or Lan arrived.

Upon entering the bank, John slowed to a deliberate walk. The lobby was lined with people. Most of them were waiting for a teller, but some were standing at tables around the edge of the room. The bank president was sitting at his desk to the right of the front door. He was separated from the rest of the room by a low rail that had a swinging gate.

"Alright, freeze," John said. "Reach. All of you, hands up." He waved his gun. "Everybody get over to that side of the room." In the well-established pattern of his previous holdups, John watched the people move toward the desk of the stunned bank president. "Now, you teller, start filling some bags with money . . . fast."

Al burst through the rear door at a dead run, his gun drawn. John started but recognized his brother in time to hold his fire.

John looked at Al. "Grab that money from the teller."

Al obediently stepped up to the teller's cage and grabbed the three bags that the teller held out to him. "Let's get out of here," Al said. His mind was obviously on the marshal's office next door.

"Not yet. We're going to take the banker along for a ransom."

"John, no." Al didn't seem too keen on the ransom schemes.

"I'm going to hold somebody for ransom." John caught movement from another teller out of the corner of his eye. "Hold it." He aimed and fired toward the movement, and the teller fell out of sight behind the cage.

"Now you'll have the marshal after us for sure," Al said.

Lan poked his head in the front door. "Hurry it up in there. There's movement in the marshal's office."

Lan bolted back outside and headed for his horse. Al was not far behind.

John brought up the rear. As he cleared the door, with his revolver aimed into the bank, the deputy marshal cleared the gap in the boardwalk between buildings. When the deputy's boot hit the wood again, John turned without delay or thought. The deputy went for his gun, and Al screamed a warning, but John sent the deputy to the ground with a well-aimed shot.

People began to fill the street from the stores and other nearby buildings.

"The bank's been robbed," somebody said.

"I heard a shot," another said.

Some of the people from the bank tumbled through the door as John made it to his horse. Men gathered around the body of the fallen deputy, and from somewhere in the crowd, a shot rang out.

Then one man mounted his horse, intent upon pursuit. But that rumpled, middle-aged man was the only one who pursued the robbers.

The outlaws raced down the rutted, dusty main street in desperate flight. With no destination in mind, each outlaw was thinking only of escape. When they cleared the edge of town, John looked back over his shoulder and cursed. "There's somebody after us."

"He probably knows his way around here," Al said. "We'll never lose him."

All four horses thundered on, leaving a cloud of dust lingering in the air.

John cursed again. "Nobody would be following us if this was Wyoming."

"There's only one," Lan said.

"Of course there's only one," John said. "There can't be more than one lunatic in this town."

"I think we'd better pick a place to jump him," Lan said.

"I give the orders around here," John said, obviously out of control.

"But I do the thinking," Lan responded.

John's face reddened, and his hand touched his gun. "When we shake this guy, I'll tend to you."

"John, listen to him," Al said. "We'll never lose this guy."

"See that spot over there by that clump of cactus?" Lan pointed where he meant, without waiting for John's permission. "John, you peel off there at the wash out. Follow it around to the left. Al and I will lead this guy in a circle that will leave you behind him, right where the broken ground starts. Got that?"

Al nodded. John didn't acknowledge.

"We'll slow down to make sure he follows me and Al."

"There's no need to kill this guy," Al said over his shoulder as his brother veered away from them. "We'll just tie him up and get out of here."

When they reached the clump of cacti, John did as he'd been instructed. Al and Lan rode into the uneven patch of ground caused by flash flooding, where the cacti took their rare gulp of water and stored it for the dry season.

Al and Lan passed the first stand of cacti, while John disappeared in the opposite direction, below the horizon of anyone on higher ground, outside the wash. The pair of riders slowed their pace, prepared to lead their adversary into the trap.

Al looked back over his shoulder to gauge the distance. "Hey, where'd he go?"

Lan looked back.

"He disappeared."

"Relax," Lan said. "It's just the uneven ground. He's just in a low spot."

Minutes went by, and no rider reappeared. "Maybe he gave up and went back to town," Al said.

"Maybe." Lan looked around. "But I didn't see him clear the wash on the far side. It doesn't seem likely that he'd give up so easily."

"Alright, gentlemen. Reach for the sky."

The voice at their backs startled Lan and Al.

"Throw down the guns," the man said.

Al complied.

"You without the gun belt. Throw down yours, too, wherever it is."

"I don't carry a gun," Lan said.

"He doesn't need one." Al bragged. "He prefers other weapons."

"Oh yeah? Like what?" asked the voice.

"He's the best fist fighter this side of the Mississippi," Al replied, daring to turn around.

The stranger showed no signs of being impressed. "That was a daring little job you did back in town." The stranger relaxed a little. "You guys got names?"

"We're the Williams Gang." Al couldn't remember ever being this dependent on the fear that name produced in Wyoming. He hoped that fear was enough to delay the man. He was proud of the reaction his name usually garnered.

"He's Al Williams. I'm Lan Phelan," Lan piped in, turning around.

"And the other—" Al said.

"Shut up," Lan said.

"Oh, I haven't forgotten the other one," the man said. "I'm keeping a lookout for him. He'll figure something is wrong. He'll be here pretty soon." The stranger grinned.

Al nodded. "Yeah, he'll be back. My brother is pretty good with a gun. You'll wish he hadn't come back."

"Oh, I'll be real careful." The man looked in the direction John had gone. "By the way, my name is Art Todd."

"Why would we care what your name is?" Lan asked.

"I'm not the law. Lucky for you, the marshal is out of town, and the deputy is in pretty bad shape from what I saw. I'm all you have to worry about." Art began to put his gun away. "I'm a safe cracker. I was casing that bank for a little withdrawal myself. I was going to hit it tonight. You boys beat me to it."

"Drop the gun, mister," John said.

When Al had quickly gathered up his own gun and the one that Art dropped, John stepped in front of the man.

"What I was about to say," Art said, obviously without much concern for his circumstances, "was that we should join forces." He smiled at the men around him. "As I see it, you're a three-man gang. You beat me out of the money in that bank. Maybe next time I'd get there first. We could go on cutting into each other's take forever . . . or we could share the work."

"For you, there won't be a next time," John growled.

"There would have been if I hadn't put myself in this position. What will you gain by killing me? Listen, you need someone who knows his way around. I have never heard of you, so you're obviously new around here."

"Never heard of us? Why I'll take you—"

"John . . ." Al grabbed John's hand before it reached the safecracker.

There was silence for a minute. Each of the men looked at the others.

Lan wondered if adding a person to the gang might help to control John. *Perhaps the addition of Art would mean more stability to the gang, and my purpose in joining up would be more closely served if we could learn more about safe burglary. Art seems smart . . . and sane.*

John's thoughts were grander. *Another man means a larger gang for me to lead. It would be another step toward fulfilling my dream.*

Finally, John stood squarely in front of Art Todd. "If we take you in, you understand that it's my gang," John said. "If I'm not around, Lan is in charge. Understood?"

He glanced at Al and Lan. John had never before talked about a second in command. There had been no need to. But this announcement, so close on the heels of his bitter words with Lan, obviously startled the other members of his gang. John had decided to give Lan authority over his own brother. That made a statement. John recognized Lan's leadership abilities, even though John hated the fact that he treasured that over his relationship with his brother.

"I can live with those terms," Art said. He smiled.

John handed Art his gun and watched warily as he holstered it. John put away his own gun, and Al followed suit. Then John stepped toe to toe with Art and slugged him in the face. The older man fell to the ground. "That's for coming after us in the first place," John said and broke into his demented laugh.

"Alright, Art," John said. "The first thing you can do for us is find us a safe place to stay. The law is bound to come looking for us sooner or later."

Art picked himself up, grabbed his chin, and began working his jaw back and forth. "Oh, you can be sure of that. Whether that deputy is dead or not, we're in lots of trouble."

Lan and Al looked at Art with puzzled faces.

"What are you getting at?" Lan asked.

"That deputy is Bill Pearson. He's very well liked around here. When people hear about him being shot, there's no telling what they'll do. I've seen it before. The whole town got together to hunt down an outlaw who tied up Pearson in order to break a buddy out of jail. I figure they'll really be up in arms about him getting shot."

"Well, I'm not worrying about that," John said. "How do you know so much? Don't the townsfolk look down on an outlaw mixing with them and their affairs?"

"They don't know I'm an outlaw." Art worked his jaw back and forth again. "I live here. I'm a safecracker, and I've never been caught. No one knows I'm responsible for some of the thefts in the area. I spread my work around so they don't pinpoint my base. It makes it look like several crooks are at work."

"That must be nice," Lan said.

"Where's the fun in that?" John smirked and then ran his hand across his seldom-tended-to beard in an absentminded movement.

"It doesn't matter." Art brought them back to the point. "We've got troubles. The marshal thinks a lot of Pearson too. He's likely to be very upset about the shooting."

"I don't care what the marshal thinks."

"Perhaps you might care what *this* marshal thinks. You've heard of Glen Herman?" Art grinned.

"The Glen Herman?" Lan asked. "He's here now?" He spun around toward John. "You've really gotten us into a mess this time."

"Glen Herman is here?" Al whispered. He shook his head.

"I ain't afraid of no big-name lawman," John said. "They all fall."

"Well, Herman doesn't like people messing around with his men," Art said. "He keeps things under control by making sure everyone knows that. You can bet he'll be after us, and he'll bring some of his deputies. He's got to prove no one can buck him in his town, or everything will get out of hand. This isn't a very civilized place. Herman has the reputation of never giving up until he's done what he set out to do."

John rolled his eyes. "He's never met the likes of me. Besides, Herman was once an outlaw himself. That's probably why he's so hard . . . You know, I wouldn't mind being a lawman." He glanced at the three men, trying to gauge their reactions. "As long as they were my laws, everything would be fine. Now, where are you going to hide us, Art?"

"I figure the best bet is to get out of Herman's way. I suggest we head for Santa Fe. He might not follow us that far. It's likely that more pressing business will keep him here." Optimism did not show in his voice. "We've got a head start."

Without verbal agreement, Lan, Art, and Al started wandering to their horses.

"Wait a minute," John said. "We came to Arizona for a reason. I'm not going to let one lousy marshal drive me out of the territory."

The other three outlaws mounted and set out on the trail eastward.

"Where do you think you're going? Get back here. I say what goes, remember?" John drew his gun and fired it over his head, but the riders kept on moving.

"Do you think he'll shoot us?" Art asked Al.

"I don't know," Al whispered. "I'm hoping we can get out of range while he thinks for a minute. Once he considers the facts of our circumstances, I think we'll be alright. Until then, we'd better keep low."

"We can't wait around here, that's for sure," Lan said to the men. "It won't be long before someone comes riding up that trail, looking for us." He nodded in the direction they had come.

The sound of thundering hooves curtailed their talk.

"Let's get moving," John quickly said. "It's a long way to Santa Fe."

BADMAN, Polzin

Days went by without mishap. The men became better acquainted, and the three others kept John from engaging in any wild activities. They passed through a string of small towns, just camps really, along the Arizona territory border. Then, unnoticed, they entered New Mexico a week after meeting Art. They followed the Rio Grande Canyon, along a route that would leave anyone who was following them with no doubt of their destination.

John was not too difficult to keep preoccupied. He was content to dream about the future and reminisce a little about the past. The mountain highlands reminded him of Wyoming. The similarity of the terrain made him think of Lander, specifically. His thoughts of Wyoming were born out by his occasional references to Marcia. He didn't mention her name, but Al understood she was the point of John's remarks. John seemed to miss Marcia more than the security of the gang's old hideout and the excitement of the old days in Wyoming.

John talked of how he would one day have a gang built around him that was so powerful and versatile that even the United States Cavalry wouldn't dare interfere. Al knew that someday, John wanted to have the rimrocks, Marcia, and more. His dream was even clearer since leaving Arizona. He wouldn't give up the past. He would return to Lander and force Marcia to fit into his way of life.

Al could not remember seeing John any more relaxed. For the first time in a while, it was possible to make suggestions to John without repercussions. Al thanked the powers of love, or whatever it was, for the peace.

⚜

Art was thrilled with the softer side John showed when he was thinking of the woman he left behind. Art soon learned that thoughts of Marcia couldn't exist side by side with thoughts of killing in John's mind, so Art felt safer when she preoccupied his mind.

Art had learned of John's ruthlessness firsthand the first day they had met, and before long, Art got to experience many tastes of John's thirst for violence.

One day, early on the trek to Santa Fe, John, as usual, was complaining about their unvaried diet. They had been eating rabbits for days and ended up in a heated discussion about how to add to their menu.

Then the outlaws happened to meet a traveler on the trail. The stranger made the mistake of being friendly to John.

"Howdy," Art heard the traveler say to John, who was leading the procession of the Williams Gang.

"Shut up," John said and whipped the man across the face with his reins as they passed.

"Hey," the man said.

"You're in our way."

Instinctively, even though he couldn't see everything that was happening, Art knew John was causing trouble again. Art got to John just as he was pushing the man from his saddle. Art grabbed John's arm in an effort to defend the stranger.

"Get out of here, Art," John said.

The stranger hit the ground, and Art dismounted to help him up. "I'm sorry, mister."

"Leave him be." John's hand went for his gun.

Art wasn't sure who he intended to shoot, him or the stranger.

Lan stepped up to John's horse and grabbed the stranger's gun from the ground, where it had fallen from its holster.

"Leave it alone, Lan," John said. "There's more than one bullet in this gun. I'm warning you."

"Knock it off, John," Lan said.

Al grabbed John's arm.

"I'm going to kill that stinking safecracker. He's crossed me too much already." John pointed his gun straight at Art.

Art felt the color draining from face as he learned he was the one in John's sights.

"Think of your gang," Lan said, taking hold of John's other arm. "You would have one less man."

John's head turned away from Art for the first time as he considered Lan's words.

The fallen man took advantage of the diversion to grab his horse's reins, lead it off, and then mount.

"He's getting away." John pointed to the stranger by nodding his head in his direction while struggling to get his arms free.

"Leave it be," Lan said.

John relaxed as the chance of stopping the man on his horse disappeared. Nothing more was said, and the outlaws went back to their horses and mounted.

Art sighed. He knew it was only Lan's ability to exert some control over John that had saved him.

The day after encountering the stranger, they entered a small town called Silver City, and John led them to the café. From his pocket, he pulled a wad of money.

"Where'd you get that?" Al asked.

"From that troublemaker back along the trail. I wasn't just pushing him off his horse. I was digging in his vest pockets. I figured he might have some money, and I was right." He waved the wad of money. "Well, I'm through with rabbits and beans. Follow me to the steak and eggs."

The others could only shake their heads. That explanation wouldn't have been forthcoming if Marcia had not been on his mind. Even so, John's explanation for attacking the man on the trail may or may not have been true.

The others hated the cruel violence John enjoyed, but they realized they might be benefitting from the reactions created by it. It helped them to be successful in their chosen career.

Eventually, the outlaws followed their leader into the café. A good meal appealed to them all.

Sometimes days of peace were followed by disruption. Once, John wandered into the lead a mile or more ahead of the others. They lost sight of him, but in the distance, they heard gunshots and knew it had to be John.

Al, Lan, and Art came to his rescue.

"Unbelievable," Lan said. "We're in the middle of nowhere, and he still gets into trouble."

The riders came over a little rise to find John standing on a flat rock, shooting into a depression a few feet away.

"What are you doing?" Lan asked. His relief was tempered by a lack of comprehension of the situation. He climbed the rock and stood beside John. He saw the answer to his question. A nest of rattlesnakes was writhing and crawling over itself. Some of them lay dead and motionless.

"Watch how they fly when I hit them," John said. His next bullet tore into one of the larger snakes and lifted it off the ground. It fell in a heap as John cackled.

Lan fought back his revulsion as he brushed past Al and Art, who were coming to take a look for themselves.

Lan shook his head. Sometimes John was restless and nothing could prevent him from finding some kind of trouble to get into. Occasionally, he behaved himself for a considerable length of time. It all depended on how he was feeling and what he was thinking about at the time. Circumstances had very little to do with his behavior.

～◎ ◎◟～

With Santa Fe still a couple of days away, Al had plenty of time to think. The sudden rise of Lan to second in command puzzled and insulted Al. He had to admit that Lan was more successful at intervening in John's plans than he could remember anyone else being. Not even when John's mind was on Marcia did Al dare suggest things the way Lan did. *How is Lan still alive after challenging John so many times?*

Al knew Lan's gunless state was a constant irritant to John. He called it gutless and indefensible; yet John respected Lan in a mysterious way. Lan even made occasional open statements of his concern for John's mental state, but after some blustering, John, inexplicably, let it blow over every time.

Lan was smart. There was no doubt about that. Still, it hurt to have his brother pick someone else over him. But all in all, Al was satisfied with things as they were. If Lan could win John's respect and be allowed a tempering role, Al would be better off than he would be as second in command.

Al wondered if John realized that Lan possessed the abilities he did not—the abilities that would make the realization of his dreams possible. Lan had intelligence and conservative ways that were sometimes needed. His influence had a settling effect on their operations. They became more like a gang. John's inconsistency was tempered by Lan. There was still recklessness, but there was more planning. Lan's influence had gotten them out of a fix on several occasions. They also had become more organized, with each member more closely filling a specific need.

Al found the more secure brand of excitement to his liking. Being an outlaw was less hard to swallow. For the first time since childhood, he could see a future. His future was still linked to John, but it was a picture he had never been able to see before. It made it easier for him to accept Lan's superior position in the gang.

John wanted to lead a large and powerful gang. Lan was helping John toward that goal—one he would probably never reach without someone like Lan at his side. Al knew they would need the help of at least a couple of others.

"Marcia will be proud of me someday," John suddenly said. His voice was soft and reverent.

Sensing John's faulty thinking, Al tried to say the appropriate thing, even though he wished John would behave in a way that Marcia could be proud of. "You don't need Marcia. You told her 'good-bye' a while back, remember?"

"I know, but I didn't mean it," John said.

Al was headed into dangerous territory, and he knew it. "You need someone who shares your dreams . . . someone who thinks like you."

"Marcia will be there. She just needs to see she can be proud of me. I don't want any other woman . . . except for other purposes." John chuckled. Even his laughter was softer when Marcia was the subject. "There's more to Marcia than that. I love her."

Al knew that John couldn't have both Marcia and his dream. And his chances of obtaining his goal as a powerful outlaw were much better than those of achieving happiness with Marcia. Even the chances of being a successful outlaw were slim, given John's temperament.

While Al had never experienced love, he refused to recognize what John and Marcia had as genuine love. It was too one-sided. *Love is sacrificial. One person puts the other person's interests above his or her own. Marcia loved John, but John certainly doesn't love Marcia. He just loved the idea of Marcia. John would be much happier fulfilling his dream for the Williams Gang, and that is something I can help him with.*

"Well, I'm a lot happier than I was in Wyoming," Al said out loud.

"I'm not." John looked at his brother. "But we've got time."

"We are staying in nicer hotels and eating well—what's not to like about that?"

"Good point."

The private thinking and personal conversations were interrupted when they neared Santa Fe. From the camp where the four men were planning to spend the night before entering town, John watched a train slowly meander along its steel tether. He watched until it was far off and then dropped from sight.

"I wonder what a train passing through here would have onboard?" John said. He looked from face to face around the fire.

"There's a little silver mine around here, up in the mountains," Art said. He swirled the coffee is his cup. "Remember, that last town was called Silver City."

"*Heavy* silver," Lan said. He was obviously making an attempt to derail the thoughts John was having, but it was too late. John already had his plan in motion.

"There might be someone worth holding for ransom."

"What is with you and kidnapping?" Lan asked.

"Maybe there are some important people on board. There must be some mine executives, bankers, or maybe even railroad officers traveling this line. We could just rob them and have a huge take."

John was silent for a minute. "OK, it's decided then. When we spot the next train, tomorrow, we jump it and clean out the passengers."

Lan breathed a sigh of relief. He was glad John had abandoned the kidnapping idea and was just set on hitting a train. "Yeah, there ought to be another eastbound train at least by this time tomorrow. We can camp here until then."

"Well, it's getting dark," John said. "Let's hit the sack."

The next morning, Lan laid out the plan in detail. "If we rush the train from the side, we can mount it while it is still moving. That way, we might be able to get on the train, get the job done, and get off before everyone knows anything has happened. If we stop the train, we have to cope with the whole train crew."

"We've got no cover for an ambush, that's for sure," Al said.

"If there are any guards, we can immobilize them before they can signal the engineer or anyone. We have to make sure we are behind the head of the train, so we can't be seen by the men running the locomotive. After we clean out the people on board, we jump and round up our horses. That old Iron Horse will just keep winding its way off into the distance, and we'll make off undetected with all the loot. By the time the passengers can spread the alarm, we'll be miles away."

"And the good thing about this is that the loot will be light and small—easy to handle, stuff like watches, rings, jewelry, and cash. It might not be a lot, but it'll be a pretty trouble-free robbery."

"It sure doesn't beat burglary," Art said. He obviously was hoping for a bigger score.

John's sneered, stopping any further discussion.

No train passed by the next day. The following day, however, they spotted one moving from west to east. An eastbound train seemed more likely to be carrying a full load of passengers.

With everything to their liking, the robbery began.

"If we get split up, we'll meet in Santa Fe," John told the others.

Lan had suggested that no one would expect them to follow the train they had just robbed to the town where the robbery would be reported. They would wear masks, change clothes after the hit, and then hide among the people of Santa Fe while they were told about the train holdup. Lan also suggested they refrain from using their real names in the hold up.

"You guys think this is all nice and safe, but remember, I'm a safe cracker. This all sounds extremely risky to me," Art said. It was the only complaint, aside from John's discomfort with the lack of sufficient excitement.

"You are about to broaden your horizons, Art," John said. "You'll love taking chances. It's exciting . . . unless you'd rather I just shoot you right now." John laughed. "OK, gang, let's go."

Al and Lan approached the train from its left. John and Art rode toward the right side as the train moved forward.

"Jump," John said to Art as they neared the rear car.

One by one, they left their horses, clinging to various parts of the car. Just as Al, the last to make it to the train, leaped from his horse, a shot rang out behind them.

"What?" Al said.

"Forget the robbery," Lan said. "Save yourself."

Thoughts of who the intruders were flashed through Art's head as each outlaw sought his own route to safety.

"Must be a posse or something," Lan said. He looked back. There was a band of riders gaining on the train, now shooting with regularity.

Art was closer to the front of the train and noticed that his horse had not yet fallen enough off the pace to clear the last car. The panic in his body propelled him through the frightened passengers in the car, to the rear landing. He dove for his horse and landed awkwardly. The muscles in his groin burned, but he was able to scramble into the saddle. As he straightened himself up and reined to the right, he found Lan at his side, with Al on the same mount.

"I'll bet they're Glen Herman's boys," Art said. "I bet they've been trailing us the whole time."

Al's mind was too jumbled to reply. He was lucky to be riding on Lan's horse. His own horse had come to a halt when the train passed it. Al had dropped to the ground and rolled away from the wheels of the railroad car. He'd then looked up to see Lan and his horse bearing down on him. Leaning far over in the saddle, Lan had grabbed Al's arm. By hanging on to the arm and hooking his leg over the horse's back, Al was able to swing himself up behind Lan.

Lan was obviously intent upon finding a way out of their predicament. "Al, get down," Lan said. The clopping of the horse's hooves and the clacking of the train wheels made it difficult for Al to hear him.

The other riders were close enough that the Al could see glints of sunlight reflecting off of their badges.

"Where's John?" Al asked.

The burst of gunfire from behind them cut off Lan's words as he started to answer.

Al sat upright in the saddle, looking for his brother.

"Get down." Lan said. He reached behind to force Al to do so.

"Where's my brother?"

"I don't know. But first we need to survive. Then we can look for him."

The train slowed to a stop, and the crewmen peered out, along with the passengers, at the scene unfolding around them. The outlaws, now some distance from the tracks, passed the head of the train. Art's horse, with its lighter burden led the way.

Al managed to turn and fire back at the posse, who continued firing at the outlaws.

The posse had been riding their horses at a fast pace much longer in an effort to catch up with the outlaws. As a result, they soon fell back from the fresh mounts they were chasing.

"I think we'd better continue on into Santa Fe, like we planned," Lan said. "As soon as we can't be seen, we need to get rid of the masks and any clothing that might be recognized."

"You don't think they know it's us?" Al asked.

"I don't know. But why take chances?"

"Do you think they got John?"

"Right now, all I'm worried about is us. Art, do you know any place around here to hide?"

Art shook his head. "Nope. I've never been to Santa Fe."

"Well, luckily, John left us a little money for ourselves, for once. We'll spend the night in a hotel and be comfortable. That's as good a cover as any, I guess—if we play it cautious. Maybe, if the posse expects us to be running, they won't be sticking around here to look for us. We'll sit tight for a while and then figure out what our next move should be." Lan spoke with authority.

"It'll be to find John." Al said. He wanted to insert his own authority, even though he didn't have much in the gang. But still, it was his brother. He should have some say in when or how they went about finding him.

"We'll see," Lan said.

There was no longer any trace of their pursuers, so they slowed their horses to a walk and allowed them to cool down.

"You sound like you think John is dead," Al said. A tear formed in his eye, and he quickly wiped it away before anybody could see it.

"We don't know that he isn't," Lan said. "We've got to take that possibility into consideration." He sounded as though he was trying to make his voice sound as compassionate as possible.

Al understood that if the posse caught up with John, he probably was dead. Al shook off the thought. "I won't put up with this," he said.

"Even if we find John tomorrow, we have to have plans," Art ventured to Al.

"John would expect that of us," Lan added.

Al made no further comment.

After they had spent a few hours picking their way through the countryside, the outskirts of Santa Fe came into view. When they reached the first buildings, the horses came to a halt, and Lan dismounted. "Riding into town double might raise some curiosity," he said. "Besides, it might be better if we didn't all appear at the same time. We can pretend not to know each other if we choose to play our cards that way."

Art and Al left Lan and walked their mounts on into town. Lan was going to wait a little while and then start walking in that direction too.

Art and Al stopped in front of a large building that had a sign out front: "The finest hotel in Santa Fe." They hitched their horses outside and, within a minute, were inside the doorway.

"We're going to have to do something about another horse," Art said. "I think we probably have enough money to buy one."

Al said nothing as they approached the hotel desk.

"Imagine how John would react if he knew we were going to *buy* a horse," Art said. He regretted trying to make the joke the minute it came out of his mouth.

"Shut up," Al replied.

"I didn't mean anything—"

"Just about everything of value we had was in John's saddlebags. They're still on his horse, wherever it is."

"Shhh. Keep it quiet. We don't want to stir up any excitement here."

Al nodded, obviously understanding.

Just as they leaned against the desk, waiting for a clerk to notice them, Lan entered through the hotel door.

"It's about time you boys got here."

Art and Al swiveled around to face the booming voice coming from behind a potted plant.

Art reached for his gun, and Lan, with clenched fists, made a quick movement to the scene where the men were. But Al recognized the faked voice.

"John!"

"You boys ought to try the train," John teased as he stepped out from behind the plant.

Al wrapped his brother in his arms. "John, John, John, I thought you were . . ." Al nearly wept.

"Dead?" John filled in with a smile.

"How did you get here?" Lan asked.

"How did you get away?" Art added.

"Well, I found myself on the landing of the last car when everything broke loose. So I just tucked my pistol into my belt and threw the gun belt away. I took off my mask and entered the car. The passengers were all bunched up together toward the front of the car. Their eyes were glued to the windows, watching the action outside. I saw you guys ride by. I didn't think to wave, sorry."

"But how did you get here? Do you mean you just rode the train in?" Art looked amazed.

"Yes, I just acted like a passenger. I joined in all excited, just like everyone else. Nobody noticed me."

"We weren't quite as lucky as you, I'm afraid," Lan said. "We had all those lawmen on our tails, and me and Al were riding double. We managed to get away from them somehow, but I'll tell you, it was pretty scary."

"Shhh," John whispered as the clerk approached the desk. "Let's get rooms, and then we can talk."

Lan paid for two rooms, and the men started up the stairs.

"All our money was in your saddlebags, John," Lan said. "All except the little bit we carry on us."

"Yeah, I wonder where that horse is. We'll need another one . . . or two, it looks like." John scratched his chin.

"We'll have to steal them," Lan said. "I'd sure like it better if we didn't have to cause a fuss around here, though."

"I've got a little money of my own," Art said. "But only enough to buy one horse."

"You holding out on us?" John glared at Art.

"It's money I had before. But we can use it to get a horse." Art's meekness seemed to be a newly acquired trait that dealing with John had taught him.

John paused. "Well, we need more than one horse anyway. I'll have to think of something."

The other outlaws looked at each other and kept walking in silence.

They reached one of the rooms and entered it. Al sat down on the bed. Art chose a chair across the room. Lan and John stood by the door.

"We can't stay here like we planned," John said. "You know why."

"We have no choice but to get our hands on some money," Lan added.

"We'll have to take care of that business and then get out of here in a hurry. If we had horses and the money from the robbery, we could stick around, but that's not the way it is."

"Anything we do is going to stir up a hornet's nest. We won't have time for anything after that happens. I don't like it." Lan looked around the group. "If we do manage to clear Santa Fe, we'll be on the run again." He finished his statement with a shrug of his shoulders and turned his palms heavenward as if to express the inevitable.

"Any ideas on how we can avoid it, hotshot?" John asked Lan.

Lan shook his head.

"Well, then let's get to it right now." John plopped down on the bed.

"Wait a minute." Art spoke up for the first time. "I'm a safecracker. There's bound to be a safe here in the hotel. We crack the safe, buy horses, and fill our stomachs. There'd be no need for us to run. Nobody would know we did it."

Everyone in the room froze. John sensed that Art's plan would not furnish the excitement he was looking forward to, but some of Lan's caution had worn off on him. Besides, diversification was one of his goals for the gang.

"Burglary doesn't raise a fuss," Art continued, his confidence with the group mounting as he sensed their acceptance of him. "Sometimes, it's a long time before anyone even knows there's been a crime." His gaze took in the growing smiles of his companions. Seeing their approval, he began to lay out his plan. "If I can get —"

"Wait a minute," John interrupted. "I'll make the plan."

"Are you saying it will be safe to rob the hotel tonight and then stick around?" Al asked.

A nervous laugh rippled through the group.

"Well, I don't know about that," Lan said. "We're strangers here and might be suspected. I think it's better we leave."

"Well, all I hope for is enough time to find a livery stable to buy some horses and to have a pleasant breakfast," Al said.

Art grinned. "We should be able to leave quietly and not be hungry anymore."

Heavier laughter erupted. John led the way and then said, "Tell us what you have in mind, Art." This gave the gang's junior member the floor.

"Well, I'd work alone. It's important to be quiet. One person will make less noise." He put out a hand to calm John's eminent interruption. "I'm less likely to be seen if I'm alone, and if I get caught, you three can still make a break for it."

"We wouldn't leave without you," Lan said. "We stick together."

"Like we did with John after the train robbery?" Al piped in.

"I like the plan," John said.

The outlaws gave their rapt attention to Art as he completed the details.

"All I need are my sensitive fingers and my ears." Art grinned. "You guys wouldn't be any help; you'd just be in the way. Just let me worry about how I do it." Art was wallowing in his acceptance by the gang. "I'll meet you back here in the room. We'll get a good night's sleep and then get up in time for breakfast. We'll stroll on down to the livery after that and be out of here while it's still morning."

John turned away.

"We've got to be careful not to be in too big a hurry," Lan said. "We're hoping that posse will pass us. We don't want to catch up to it again."

Al stood up. "I'm going to the other room to take a nap." *After all, what do they need me for? Nobody cares what I think anyway.*

Lan got up. "I'll go with you."

As they walked out the door, Al looked back at John, who had pulled a chair close to the little table in the room.

John looked at Art. "Want to play some cards, Art?"

⁓❦⁓

A few hours later, in the small hours of the morning, Art left John, Al, and Lan in a room together, waiting anxiously for his return from his solitary work in the lobby below them. Everyone knew that the hotel was locked up, so the only possible disturbance would have to come from inside.

No one was around as Art made his silent approach. He tiptoed down the stairs and scanned the lobby. The large safe was clearly visible behind the clerk's desk. He assumed the door marked "private" led to a room where the clerk could rest until morning—a benefit of having the late shift. Art thought he heard soft snoring from beyond the door. He glanced at the pigeon-hole compartments lining the wall behind the desk, some stuffed and some empty, and then approached the safe.

Art gave the huge metal case a solemn inspection. Then, satisfied it was nothing more than what it seemed, he skillfully turned the dial on the door. He carefully twisted the dial left, then right. Once he felt comfortable with the mechanism, he began deciphering the combination, unscrambling the numbers that would make the tumblers fall as needed to make the door open.

After a relatively short period of time, he was inside the safe. He selected a compartment with a sliding drawer. It contained currency, as Art had guessed. He quickly slipped a few bills out of each of the neatly banded stacks and then grabbed a few loose bills. He knew a few bills missing from a stack would not be noticed until the close of business the next day. He didn't want the theft discovered too quickly.

Keeping alert for anyone who might be in the lobby, Art quietly closed the door to the safe and gave the dial a spin. Then he started back up the stairs to the rooms with the money stuffed in his pockets. He was sure it would be enough for their purposes, yet not enough to cause the hotel to miss it immediately.

Art burst into John's room. "We're rich again." He grinned and pulled the money from his pockets, allowing it to cascade to the floor.

"Keep it down," John said. "There're people trying to sleep." He let out one of his laughs but kept it deep in his throat.

"Let's us get some sleep," Lan said. His smile was no less exuberant than those on the faces of the others.

Amid nodded agreement, the men separated and headed to their beds.

John was the last to sit down at the table in the dining room the next morning. Everyone ordered a hearty meal of eggs, bacon, pancakes, and coffee, with the exception of John. The gang's leader chose ham over bacon to preserve his individuality.

The hungry men kept conversation to a minimum and finished their meals quickly. Then Lan suggested they set off in pairs to find the livery stable. They didn't want anyone to remember them asking for directions.

The early morning peacefulness made the men edgy. It was like their guilt was visible.

"This town is awful quiet this time of day," John said. The three other men only turned to look at him, not saying anything.

As they stepped off the boardwalk into the street outside the hotel, John watched Al and Lan walk away for a moment and then erupted. "Maybe we should wake somebody up." He drew his gun and aimed skyward.

Art grabbed for the gun. "Don't be crazy."

John was furious. He turned on Art. "Nobody grabs my gun. Nobody calls me crazy." He wrenched the gun from Art's grasp and pulled the trigger. The bullet hit the boardwalk near Art's foot.

Art jumped away, yelling in fear. "What are you doing?" He held up his hand as if he were giving John a stop sign.

John paused and looked around. A few curious people popped their heads out from various establishments.

"What is going on?" Lan asked. He ran toward John.

"I guess I got carried away," John said. He looked at Art and grinned. He knew he had gone too far, but he had to make sure they understood he was still in charge.

John glanced around again. The few curious people went on their way. The entertainment was over.

"So much for not drawing any attention," Lan said. "But nobody seems to be making anything of it. How could you do something like that?"

John didn't answer.

Lan stared up and down the street and then turned to Al. "Come on, let's go find that livery stable."

Al had been watching, speechless.

John scowled, but he followed Art in the opposite direction from the one Al and Lan took.

Lan and Al found the stable in the alley just off the main street. Then Lan sent Al to get the others so that all four men could approach the stable together.

No one was in the barn when they walked in, so they tried the front door to a little office attached to it.

"Howdy," a voice said as they entered through the unlocked door.

"Howdy," John said to the unseen stranger. "We'd like to buy a couple of horses."

"Any particular kind? Pack horses? Cutting horses?"

"Any kind," John said.

Lan cautioned John and flashed a phony smile at the man.

"Yes, sir," the livery man said. "The horses are right out here." He showed the outlaws through the back doorway, into the stable.

They walked up to two average-looking, brown horses.

"These two be alright?" the man asked.

"Yeah, fine," John said. He pulled out a pack of money.

The man watched as John counted out loud.

"Twenty, thirty, forty . . . forty-five enough?"

"Sure, sure," the man said, obviously anxious to satisfy this customer. The look in his eyes said that he hadn't seen all that much paper money.

John grabbed a saddle from the stall shelf and began outfitting one of the horses.

"Wait. The tack doesn't go with the . . ."

John showed the man a look that stopped his resistance. He grabbed an empty gun belt that was hanging on a wall peg. "I could use one of these. I lost mine."

When both horses were ready, Al and John mounted and faced the other outlaws.

"Let's head for Colorado," John said. "It's a new place for us to conquer."

"We'll talk about it on the trail," Lan said. He didn't like discussing their plans in front of the stable owner. He obviously had been interested in the wad of money, which meant he would remember them.

Lan and Art went to fetch their own horses, while Al and John started out of town on theirs.

The exit from Santa Fe went well. Within a few miles, Art and Lan had recovered the ground between them and rejoined Al and John. As they picked their way along the trail, scaling the mountains between them and Colorado, they went over the events of their last few hours in Santa Fe.

"There wasn't any fuss around the hotel when we went back to get our horses," Lan said.

"There still weren't many people up and about," Art said. "It's Saturday."

"I should have shot that guy at the stable," John told Lan. "But you guys would have had kittens. He knows where we're going."

Lan looked at John. Finally, he voiced his thoughts. "It was you that shot off his mouth."

Art and Al showed terror on their faces in reaction to Lan's audacity.

"Do you still think we should go to Colorado?" Lan asked.

"It's as good a place as any," John replied. He was calm.

"But—" Lan said.

"But what?" John retorted. "I've had enough backtalk from you. I'm the boss, remember? You all seem to be forgetting that a lot lately." John yanked his gun from his holster and looked them all in the eyes. "I said we're going to Colorado. Anybody want to challenge me?"

There was no further discussion.

The Williams Gang kept a leisurely pace and spent one night camped on the trail prior to reaching their next destination.

John spent the time around the campfire complaining that the money they took from the hotel would not last long. "We spent almost all of it on horses and food at the café. We didn't buy any rations to take along, so we're back to rabbit stew and the little dried beef that Art and Lan had in their saddlebags. Before we get far into Colorado, we're gonna be hungry again and needing a comfortable place to stay."

John paused. "Since somebody was so careful not to take too much money from the safe, we've got to hit a bank along the way. There's bound to be one in the next little town we come to."

"Another high risk?" Art asked. He took a sip from his coffee to avoid eye contact with John.

"What's the matter, Art?" John sneered. "You knew what you were getting into when you joined up with us. You practically begged to get in on the action."

"I just don't believe in taking unnecessary chances." Art wanted to save face with the rest of the guys.

"You'd better watch your mouth." John shoved a piece of rabbit into his mouth. There was silence for a moment, except for the sounds of the fire crackling.

"Hold it, you two," Lan said. "John's right. We are going to need money soon. I'm not sure robbing a bank is the best way to get it . . ." Lan waved off John's objection and continued. "Remember, we don't know the status of that posse. Are they still out there, or did they give up? Are there any other lawmen looking for us?" Lan shrugged. "Are they looking for us around Santa Fe? Do they think we headed for Texas? Perhaps they guessed right, and they're following us right now. Glen Herman could still be closing in on us. We just don't know." Lan looked around the campfire circle and then straight at John.

"My guess is that the posse is still looking for us," Art said. He dumped out the rest of his coffee. "I told you Glen Herman doesn't give up when someone challenges his authority. We did worse than that; we shot one of his deputies."

"I think I only wounded him, though," John said.

"A while back, you were sure you killed him," Al reminded his brother.

John ignored him. He took another bite.

"It's only a matter of time until Herman talks to that stable owner and heads this way," Lan said. "Since we are tight for time, a quick strike like a bank holdup might be our best bet. We get some money and get out. We'll leave Herman and his posse further behind and have plenty of money for a while. All things considered, I guess a bank is the best thing."

Art and Al contemplated the idea.

"OK," Al said. "I'm in."

"Me, too," Art agreed.

"What is this, a democracy?" John looked at the other men. "Of course we'll do it — 'cause I say so."

The next morning, John went alone to scout out the bank in the next town. Spring was well along, and it definitely was a warm day. He first rode up to the hitching rail at a little café. He had a little money left and was thirsty and hungry. He clomped his way inside, sat down at a table, and then called across the room to the waitress. The place was empty, except for her, John, and an old oriental cook, who could be seen in the kitchen.

The waitress came to the table to take his order.

"Say, girlie, after you bring me my food, come and sit with me a while," John said.

The girl hesitated, looked around, and then gave John a small smile. He could see she was at least curious about him.

The waitress took John's order of ham and eggs. Then she turned it in to the cook and took John up on his offer.

"Maybe I will join you for a while before you eat," she said, "It'll give me a chance to rest my feet."

"I won't mind at all." John grinned.

"Thanks. Sometimes, it's nice to have someone to talk to—to have a little conversation."

"I ain't had any female companionship for a long time." He paused and looked closely at the girl. "Say, after I eat, how about if you and me . . ."

"Conversation is all you get, mister." The girl rose from her chair and flipped her hair over her shoulder, as if to say she regretted ever sitting down with him.

"Sure, sure. Sorry." The last word tasted peculiar in John's mouth. His uncharacteristic politeness reminded him of being with Marcia.

Just then, there was the sound of boots clomping through the doorway from the street. The girl looked up, saw something over John's shoulder, and attempted to start a lighthearted conversation. "You'd better behave yourself—here's a marshal." She obviously was joking, but she had John's attention.

John spun around to face the tall newcomer, who stood directly behind him. John's hand involuntarily came to rest on his revolver. It was a marshal alright. His badge gleamed neatly, the result of frequent polishing.

"Good morning, Mr. Williams," the marshal said. "My name is Glen Herman."

"Morning, marshal," John said. His hands felt like lead. Only the fingers of his right hand were capable of moving. They caressed the butt of his six-shooter. He did not show the terror that threatened to overwhelm him.

"I heard your name mentioned in connection with some trouble in Arizona. I telegraphed some inquiries, and guess what?"

John shrugged.

"I got a reply from a marshal in Wyoming." Herman gave John a hard look. "There's a reward for you up there. They've got wanted posters all over on you. When I started digging around, I found one of those posters myself. The drawing's not a bad likeness." He pulled a piece of paper from his vest pocket. "Want to see?"

"No, that's alright." John waved Herman's hand away. John's appearance was cool, but his stomach was churning.

"When the man you bought horses from in Santa Fe said you were headed this way, my boys and I hustled right down here, but no one had seen any strangers passing through in a group of four, so we just sat and waited. It wasn't a long wait."

"Where are your pals, Williams?" the marshal asked.

The waitress backed off, obviously expecting trouble. She leaned against the window to the kitchen.

"Now, wait a minute," John said. "I haven't done anything wrong. I don't know what you're talking about in Arizona. I just came in here to eat breakfast."

"What about Wyoming?" The marshal tugged on his hat with a confidence that showed he knew he had his man. "Come on, Williams. We've been following you. What about the train outside Santa Fe? You almost fooled us by splitting up. But we've been watching closely. Odds were good you'd pass through this town." He took a step toward the door. "We've got you now, Williams. I'm going to get the county sheriff. I'll turn you over to him for safekeeping, until I can work out travel arrangements."

Just as John considered shooting Herman in the back as he left, he got more bad news.

"I've got a deputy outside. He won't hesitate before shooting. Don't try leaving. Just finish your breakfast. I'll be back with the sheriff in a few minutes." The marshal walked out to the street.

The waitress picked up John's meal from the kitchen and served it to him, but then she kept her distance.

John jumped up from the table and ran after Herman. He caught him just beyond the café door.

"Marshal," John said. The deputy beside the door quickly intercepted John. "Marshal, I just want to talk to you a minute." He wanted the deputy to hear what he had to say.

Herman paused and turned around.

"Glen," John said, "I know you used to be on the other side of the law. I thought maybe we could work something out." John's tone of voice stayed familiar, even though the marshal's look was not encouraging. "Maybe we could join forces. I hear you have a real fast gun."

Herman just stared at John, not saying anything. There was no possibility of misunderstanding John's words. He was asking the marshal to turn outlaw again.

"Bring some of your boys along," John said. "We'd have a gang no one would dare challenge, not even the U.S. Cavalry. We'd have fast guns, brains, and all kinds of specialists. You could have all the money you ever dreamed of, and there'd be no more risk than you're taking right now as a lawman. Of course, I'd be in charge. You'd have to answer to me. What d'ya say?"

Herman spit on the ground, glanced at the deputy, and turned his face back toward John. Rage burned in his eyes. "I am a lawman. What

I used to be is not important. My job is to track down scum like you." The marshal turned away again and started down the street. Then he turned to John once more. "What makes you think I'd trust someone like you? How could I trust a man who shoots on sight, without reason? I heard about the incident with the Rivera Gang. Back in Arizona, once we figured out who you were, all kinds of stories surfaced. I would never be able to turn my back to you. If I were to turn outlaw again, it wouldn't be to join you."

John glared at the marshal and then watched him stride toward the sheriff's office.

"If you aren't going to eat your breakfast, you might as well come along now," the deputy said to John, obviously mindful that the marshal's back was to the outlaw.

John reached for his gun and placed his hand on it. The deputy started to protest and then stopped. John figured the deputy didn't want to lose the advantage by wrestling with him. They stepped into the street, John a step ahead of the deputy, and followed in the marshal's footsteps.

When they arrived at the sheriff's office, just a few hundred yards down the street, the sheriff was waiting for them. Herman had warned him that Williams would be coming.

Herman sent the deputy to round up the other members of the posse, who were spread out searching for the Williams Gang. It appeared there was not going to be any warfare.

The sheriff sized up the man the marshal had told him was a dangerous outlaw. John Williams didn't look as mean or crazy as the marshal said he was.

The sheriff had his own problems. The Lincoln County war was raging. Ranchers and outlaws like Billy the Kid were making it difficult to keep the peace. Sheriff Pat Garrett had his hands full down in Santa Fe, but he would take a dozen men like John Williams before he would choose to deal with Billy.

"After we get this one locked up, we'll go find the rest of them," the marshal said to the sheriff.

But John Williams was not yet in a cell and still had his revolver. As the two lawmen stood facing each other and talking, John saw his chance and quickly drew his gun. He fired twice before either the marshal or the sheriff could react. Their bodies crumpled to the floor, and John ran for the street. The recently departed deputy was nowhere in sight. John jumped on a horse that was standing in front of the sheriff's office and headed out at top speed.

From a distance, the rest of the gang saw John returning in a hurry. It was obvious that something was wrong. So they were all mounted and ready to ride when John reached them.

"I'll tell you about it later," John said. He panted and put his hands on his knees. "Just get out of here as fast as you can."

"Where are we heading?" Lan asked.

"It's every man for himself right now. It's better we split up for a while. I'll head north for now. We'll meet in Trinidad after everything dies down a little, in say, two months."

There was no reason for them to question his reasoning. The men divided, and the horses spread out in all directions, at a rapid pace.

John urged his horse through the scattered rocks of the hills bordering the Rio Grande and climbed the crests of the higher peaks, starting miniature landslides along the way. In the afternoon heat, he and his horse began to sweat heavily.

They finished the last climb and started a temporary descent. John paused long enough to look back over the terrain he had covered. In the distance, he spotted a group of riders heading in his direction. Undoubtedly, the posse knew he was headed over the mountain pass.

John turned his mount down the forward side of the hill and began picking his way to the ravine below. There would be no way to maintain visual contact with his pursuers, and he hoped that would not lull him into assuming he was outdistancing them. Conversely, they would not be able to keep him in sight either.

He forced himself to push his horse at a dangerous pace, considering the treacherous terrain and the heated condition of the horse. He wanted to put as much distance between his adversaries and him as possible. He hoped he could use their inability to make visual contact to shield his change of direction in a maneuver designed to confuse the posse and make them doubt their own assumptions of his destination.

If he made it to Trinidad, he would cherish his success in convincing them he had gone elsewhere. His success might be temporary, but he couldn't think of a reason the posse would expect him to head there if his tactics worked to confuse them. If he wasn't successful and was caught or killed, there would be no point in worrying.

Maybe they'll pick up someone else's trail, he thought hopefully. He'd gladly sacrifice the life of one of the other members of his gang for his own life. He pressed on toward the next steep incline.

A few days after John arrived in Trinidad, he spent his last few coins on a meal. While relishing every bite he took, he overheard four men at the café discussing what sounded like a possibility for John to fill his pockets, and his stomach.

"You see, we ride in there at night, bump off any sentries, and drive the whole herd up into the canyon," one of the rustlers said to the others. "We spend the rest of the night changing brands and dividing the herd into smaller bunches. Then we drive the small herds separately to the Kansas and Pacific railhead. The K and P is new and just itching to get any business they can, so they don't ask too many questions. We're just moving a herd to the railhead—perfectly legal. Each of us will have a small herd." The man, apparently the leader of the gang, looked around at the faces of his followers. "Well, how do you like it?"

"I like it just fine," John said from the next table.

The rustlers scooted their chairs back in surprise, realizing they had been overheard. The leader's hand was on his gun.

"Don't worry. My name is John Williams. I'm not the law. Quite the contrary; I'd like to join up." John stood up and moved closer to the other table. "I'm out of money, and your little deal sounds like a good way for me to keep fed and you to get an extra hand. I'd love to take care of those sentries for you personally." The old excitement was returning.

"I don't know that we want to cut the take up another way," the leader said. "You're not the law, huh? What line are you in?"

"I do a little of everything," John bragged, "except anything legal." He laughed. "I've never tried rustling, but killing sentries is right in my line."

"We don't necessarily have to kill them . . ." the leader said.

"Now I remember." Another rustler spoke up. "John Williams, you're the guy who shot one of his own gang up in Wyoming."

"You mean that Rivera guy?" John said. "That wasn't my gang."

The leader of the rustlers took over the conversation. "We could use another man, but not a traitor. What's your story on the Rivera thing?"

"Well, that guy was turning to run. He would have left us short a gun, and we would have been outnumbered in a shootout."

"So you shot him?" another rustler said. "That doesn't make sense. You still ended up short one gun. One gun wouldn't have made that much difference. I heard you shot him for no reason. There was no shootout."

A blond man chimed in. "I hear you like to do that."

John fumbled for an answer, but the rustlers' leader spared him the trouble of telling another lie.

The leader looked down to admire his fancy boots and said, "I think we ought to take a chance on him." He seemed to be asserting that he was superior to the threat John might pose. "You're just the kind of man we need. If you make any trouble, we'll make you regret it. Any objections?"

Shoulders shrugged all around. The tension broke.

"Alright. I guess you're in," the large man said. "My name is Slade." He extended his hand.

That night, five men rode onto a ranch not far from town and closed in on the herd of cattle.

"Cut that group there out," Slade said to John.

John followed orders.

"Run down that lead steer," another man said.

John headed off the first steer in line and turned him.

"You're pretty good at that, for a green horn," Slade said.

"I'm just disappointed there weren't any sentries," John replied.

Before long, they had turned the herd in the direction they desired.

"That'll do it," Slade said. "Now, let's get them to the canyon."

There was only a friendly dog to ward off predators, and the outlaws easily drove the cattle to a canyon that had been chosen for the branding and separating. The rustlers had targeted a small ranch because it probably would not have enough ranch hands to ward off the outlaws at night. Only the yapping of the dog and the lowing of the herd disturbed the silent darkness.

However, long before daylight, the rustlers heard thundering hooves clomping in their direction. As the horses got closer, the outlaws could hear the ranchers talking among themselves.

"It's a good thing that Buster was alert enough to bark and carry on the way he did," one of the ranchers said to another one. "And these tracks are pretty easy to follow. Even in the dark, a whole herd leaves a pretty obvious trail."

The rustlers were trapped in the canyon, and the ranchers were approaching from the only open end. They ran for cover, searching for a way to escape, but they found neither. If they were found with the herd, it was over for them.

The rustlers and their pursuers all reached the same conclusion at once, and gunfire erupted from a dozen barrels. The moonlight presented just enough of the outlines of the ranchers to make them targets. One rustler mounted his horse, trying to make a run for it. He was picked off by a bullet.

John knew that staying to fight was not the smart thing to do—the odds were heavily against them. They were outnumbered and trapped. He moved silently away from the other outlaws, hiding behind his horse. When he was at a safe distance, he left his horse behind.

While the gunfight raged and the cattle milled around nervously, on the verge of stampeding, John struggled to escape up the walls of the canyon. Grasping bushes and rocks, slipping precariously on loose dirt, desperately scrambling for his life, he managed to reach the top of the canyon wall in a few minutes. The noise below covered the sounds of his grunts and the small rockslides he caused.

He looked down and saw that the rustlers had stopped returning gunfire. They had surrendered, or more likely, they probably were all dead. He could hear the ranchers yelling orders to one another, but he couldn't make out their exact words.

John refused to think of his retreat as cowardice. The last moments with the Rivera Gang came to mind. His escape was smart tactical thinking. Fighting would have been useless, as the others found out. His one gun wouldn't have made much difference. He knew he had to get away fast, before the ranchers discovered they had one more horse than body, or captive rustler, and began looking for the missing man.

Lying at the top of the canyon, catching his breath, John cursed. "It's going to be a long walk to anywhere. I might as well get going."

On the run once again, he realized he missed Lan and Art and, of course, his brother, Al. One more thought entered his mind: Marcia. *Sweet, loving Marcia.* Yes, he missed her most of all. He missed her more than all the others put together. His mind could focus on the good and ignore the truth of their relationship. *There is a good chance I will never see her again. My situation is not promising—on foot, miles from a town, with hunters on my trail. But if I'm going to die, it will be trying to reach Marcia. I have to go somewhere, so I might as well head back to Wyoming.*

When daylight broke, John was as far from the rustler operation as his two feet could manage. With more distance between him and the canyon, his thoughts became more orderly. He calmed himself into the demeanor he always took on when he thought of Marcia. He realized he would face other problems, besides the ranchers behind him. At least their search would probably be short-lived. His gang would be waiting for him in Trinidad, he had the problem of traveling to Lander without a horse, and he didn't want to be hunted as a horse thief while leading a posse to Marcia's place. Horse theft was more serious than rustling. Still, a cowboy without a horse was lost, so any pursuit would be more intense.

One problem he didn't want to think about, but knew he needed to, involved the Ute Indians, who were unfriendly toward white men. The mountains were not safe to travel. The Utes were upset by the activity of the Kansas and Pacific Railroad because the tracks were being laid across their land without their permission. The Union Pacific was having the same trouble further north. Red Cloud's treaty wasn't the Ute's treaty. White man's surrender of Fort Kearny hadn't done anything for them. It was only good for the Sioux. Besides, the ranchers in Wyoming hardly treated the Utes fairly in any respect. The objection of the tribe was met with bloodshed. Thus, a perpetual state of war existed.

John knew that if he didn't trek through the mountains, he faced hunger, possible capture, and more. But if he ever wanted to see Marcia again, he would need to press on. He convinced himself that he had to do it out of love. If he didn't succeed, he was no worse off than if he didn't try. He didn't even allow himself to think about what would happen when he reached her.

He shook Marcia from his mind and hobbled through morning light on weary legs, feeling every one of his scrapes and bruises from climbing the canyon wall.

After another day and a night spent on his feet, John sought shelter that did not include a bed of needles under an evergreen tree. That's when he happened across a ranch. It was secluded, and it reminded him of Marcia. He had thought about her more since the trap in the canyon than he had for months, and that was saying something. Once the immediate danger was over, she was almost all he thought about.

At the ranch, John stole a horse and left unnoticed. He pushed the horse, aware only of his desire to get back to Wyoming as quickly as possible. He no longer thought about whether or not his life was in danger or about the rest of his gang.

During his journey, John encountered no trouble with Indians or white men. He spent his days climbing the hills on the east side of the continental divide, fording numerous streams along the way. He only stopped when he could no longer go on without rest. He prepared the food he found along the way and ate it quickly so he could continue his journey early each morning.

"Bah, rabbits and birds," he said to himself. "I've seen enough rabbits and birds for a lifetime." His loneliness wore on him. He would be the last to admit it, but he needed other people in his life.

Finally, he reached Wyoming. He was approaching a gathering of trees on the edge of a small clearing, near a creek, when movement caught his eye, followed by violent noises in the near distance. Instantly on his guard, John dismounted and shuffled closer. He saw three familiar figures thrashing about and yelling. Their horses were standing nervously at the water's edge, drinking between starts caused by the outbursts.

It was Art, Lan, and Al. They were alive. It was more than John had let himself hope. Lan had Art backed up against a tree and was swinging his fists, while Art protested and protected himself as well as he could.

John walked into sight. "Lan, what's going on here?"

They stopped, and their mouths hung open.

"John, you're alive!" Al said. Al ran toward his brother.

"Of course I'm alive." John waved a hand and backed away from Al's advance. "I want an explanation." Even he noticed the strength in his voice. He felt happier than he had been since the day he was separated from his gang.

Lan spoke up for the group. "Well, Art was going on about you being dead, and it was bothering Al . . ." he began.

"Go on," John said.

"Well, he said it didn't surprise him—given the way you are always so careless and all . . ."

"And your little brother started pushing me around, screaming at me," Art said. He stepped in front of Al to plead his case. "I was just defending myself, and then Lan stepped in."

"Art, when John is gone, I'm in charge," Lan said.

"If John's dead, I don't have to obey his second-in-command." Art turned to John. "If you're dead, there isn't a Williams Gang, or at least, not one I want to be part of."

"Listen, when I'm gone, Lan's in charge. No arguments. You hear that too, little brother?" John said.

Silence hung in the air for a moment, and then John spoke again. "So, you gave me up for dead, huh, Art?"

"Well, things were screwed up real bad. I didn't see how you could still be alive."

John pushed Art against a tree and grabbed him by the collar. "You don't worry about whether I'm dead or alive. Your job is to take orders. If I am alive, and I find out you've deserted or done any foolish thing like that, I'll come looking for you and kill you." Memories of the Rivera Gang and the rustlers came flooding into John's mind.

Art lowered his head and backed away without a word.

"What are you doing here?" John asked Lan. He looked at Art in disgust and amusement, looked at the other members of his gang intensely, and then spat on the ground before Lan could reply.

"We waited in Trinidad for a little while, and when you didn't show up, we thought, well, I thought, we should head back to the old hideout," Lan said.

John looked at Art again and spat once more, still seething at the weakness of loyalty in the safecracker. "You're lucky I wasn't there, Art. You would be dead." His words were only half in response to Lan's explanation. He turned to Lan. "You boys sure waited an awful long time in Trinidad." He was being sarcastic, and he knew they would pick up on that.

As John looked around the circle of men, it seemed to grow larger, even though no one had moved. He continued. "No further discussion of Lan's leadership or words concerning his decision to leave Trinidad so soon is necessary. If there is a need, Lan and I will talk about it later, on our own. Is everything clear now?"

All three nodded their heads.

"Alright, I don't want to see this sort of thing again. Come on, we're heading back to Lander."

Art opened his mouth. John glared at him.

"I was just going to warn you about the Utes," Art said.

"I know about them," John retorted.

Lan joined in the conversation. "The mountains just west of here are crawling with hostiles. It would be good to stay east of the mountains."

"I know that," John said.

Lan sighed. He seemed to fear saying any more.

"I'm not a violent man, you know." Art needed to apologize to clear his guilty conscience. He was concerned about his image and his standing with John. "But when Al started shoving me —"

"Enough," John said. "That conversation is finished. "Let's head north. We'll stay east of the Utes. The Arapaho won't bother with us." He walked away and grabbed the reins of his horse.

As the foursome picked its way through the trees, time relieved the tension, and conversation developed.

"John, you never told us what you've been doing or where you've been," Al said. He was riding next to John.

"I'll tell you about it some other time," John said. "What happened to you guys?"

"We made the mistake of going into the mountains," Art said. *Maybe this will help John understand that Lan's decision-making ability isn't everything he thinks it is.*

"We were caught in the middle of the Lincoln County cattle war." Lan shrugged. "We headed for the mountains to get out of that mess and ran smack into an Indian raid on a railroad camp. When the smoke cleared, we were the only ones around who were still alive." Lan made a point to turn sideways to stare at Art. "How was I supposed to know what was going to happen? The only reason we survived is that we dug ourselves into the ground and covered up. Otherwise, we'd be dead, like everybody else."

"Good thinking," John said.

"We also ran into the railroad crew near the Colorado-New Mexico line." Lan drifted into reverie. "When the Kansas and Pacific finishes their work and the Atcheson, Topeka, and Santa Fe completes its expansion, the Chisholm Trail will be obsolete." Lan looked up for a minute. "I guess it'll take a little longer now to get that work done, because of the Indians . . ."

"The Utes shouldn't be bothering any railroads, except the U.P.," John said.

"A railroad is a railroad to the Indians," Lan said. "Besides, the Apaches are restless too. They were pretty good boys, those railroad men—except for the coolies, of course." Lan paused again. "They're all dead now."

"What are you going on about?"

"It was the Chiricahuas that wiped out the railroad camp. If we hadn't dug in, we either would have been killed outright or burned in the fire they set."

"We stayed around to bury the bodies and clean up a little," Al said. "Then we headed this way, where you found us."

"Those railroad men were nothing to us," John said. "So don't go whimpering about them." His horse stumbled lightly on a loose stone, drawing John's attention. "How did you find each other?"

"Well, John, it was kind of like the way you found us—by accident," Al said.

"We were all on the trail to Trinidad, and we eventually wound up in the same place at one time or another," Art said.

"Now, what happened to you, John?" Al asked.

John smiled. "Well, I was out of money, and I overheard some guys planning to rustle some cattle. I joined up with them." John shook his head. "They're probably all dead now. Boy, that was a mistake. We raided a ranch, and the ranchers came looking for us right away. They trapped us in a canyon, where we were altering the brands. The other guys stayed and fought it out. I headed for the top of the canyon wall and got out. I think all the others got killed. I never even got anything for my trouble. I didn't want to go back to Trinidad after that. I made other plans."

Nobody said anything for a few minutes. They passed through a stream where fish were jumping. A couple of them mentioned stopping to catch a few fish for dinner later that night, but they wanted to keep pressing on while they still had daylight.

"We got a few things from the railroad camp—rings, gold teeth, and a little money," Lan said. "Not much, but we did eat well while we were waiting in Trinidad." Lan blinked back the memory of the slaughter.

"At least you didn't forget to check their pockets this time." John laughed. "Speaking about food, do you realize how little I have had to eat in the past few days?" John rubbed his belly. It was obvious no answer was required. "Give me something out of your grub," John said. "Then, let's hightail it to the next town so I can have a real meal. I'm really hungry."

Al wet his lips with his tongue as he reached into his saddlebag to give John a chunk of jerky. The younger brother braced himself to ask a touchy question. "Are you going to see Marcia when we get back?"

John looked back over his shoulder and slowed his horse. He waited for Al to come alongside him. "Yes, after we get to the hideout, I'll go see her."

They found no town that night, so they ate from the remaining stock of food in their saddlebags and stopped for some rest. They didn't hold their customary campfire chat. Instead, each man was silent with his own thoughts, and they crawled into their bedrolls early.

When daylight appeared, they were already mounted and winding their way through the low hills. Near midday, they stopped at the edge of a low valley. They looked down into the valley and saw a camp of railroad workers. The Chinamen, in their coolie hats, easily distinguishable among the workers, talked loudly. The noise of their foreign tongue wafted up to outlaws on the side of the hill.

John quietly mentioned the idea of joining the railroad men to beg for a meal, but then he decided it would be better to remain unnoticed. There were enough people looking for the Williams Gang. Besides, John didn't want to be caught in an Indian raid. A railroad camp was a prime target.

Lan looked out at the camp in the valley and sighed as he remembered the last time he looked down on a railroad camp. Belonging to the Williams Gang had shown Lan a fair amount of bloodshed, but nothing compared to the slaughter at that camp.

The gang skirted the camp and headed west, toward the higher mountains. After commenting that he knew it would not be safe for white men to seek refuge on higher ground, John led the gang into the hills for only a short while and then headed east again. They all preferred to take their chances with white lawmen instead of red-skinned warriors.

BADMAN, Polzin

The Williams Gang's hideout was still intact and apparently undiscovered. Only a few rodents and lizards disturbed the stillness. The outlaws settled in for an indefinite stay, and the next day, John went to see Marcia.

The little ranch house on the edge of the clearing still looked the same. In reality, nothing had changed much, but in John's mind, everything was different.

When he reached the house, John tied the horse to the hitching rail out front and stepped onto the porch. There was no need to decide whether or not to knock, for Marcia met him at the door, as always. She was wearing a beautiful blue print dress. John wondered if she always looked like that or if she'd hurried into her fancy clothes when she saw him coming. He'd never seen her look any less tidy.

They fell into an embrace. Apparently, all animosity, real or imagined, was forgotten on both sides. Marcia's body felt as soft as John remembered. He pushed her slightly away and gave her a kiss—a kiss that told her he was sorry he had left.

Marcia turned toward the open door to the ranch house and motioned John to go in. "There's someone here I would like you to meet," she said. Her inflection was pleasant, raising no fear on John's part. But he was curious.

He entered the front room and saw a small, fragile-looking, young woman seated in a rocking chair. She was almost as pretty as Marcia.

"John, this is Cathy Herman," Marcia said. "I believe you met her husband."

John stopped, and his eyes got big. He had been betrayed by his love.

"She says you killed him. I didn't believe it, but I can see by your expression that it's true."

"Sit down, John," Cathy said. "I want to talk to you." She motioned for him to sit in the chair across from her. She was calm—much calmer than John would have expected.

John looked around like a caged animal. He saw no one else. He eased into the chair, wondering what he was in for. "How did you find me?" he asked.

Cathy rocked back and forth a couple of times before speaking. "Glen and his deputies knew you were from around here. The people in Lander know you have a hideout somewhere up in the hills. They didn't know if you were up there or not, but I decided to stay in Lander a while so that I could have a chance to see you. I left word that I was looking for you, peacefully, and eventually, Marcia came to me."

The explanation seemed simple enough. Still, John was terrified by the apparently easy-to-follow trail he had left.

"I'm surprised no one has used her to get to you before," Cathy echoed his thoughts aloud. She paused. "It would be a shame if someone did. She's a very nice woman. You should appreciate her more than you apparently do."

Marcia pulled up a chair and made a shushing sound. In John's eyes, the blush on her cheeks only heightened her beauty. But he couldn't afford to get too distracted. He had to figure out what Cathy was thinking.

After a longer pause, she answered the unasked question. "Let me explain why I've been trying to reach you, John," Cathy began. "You see, Glen used to spend his time in much the same way you do now—as an outlaw. He was always running and hiding and gambling with his life. However, not too long after we met in a hotel saloon where I was working, I persuaded him to give himself up to the law and go straight. He helped the law round up some pretty vicious criminals, and the governor showed his appreciation. Glen spent some time in prison, but eventually, he was released. That was in Arizona territory. Eventually, Glen became a lawman himself, as you know."

John tapped his right foot up and down. *Is she really about to ask me to give up the only lifestyle that makes me feel alive?*

"Because of his love and devotion for me, he changed his life, dedicating himself to making amends for the wrongs he had done," Cathy continued.

She maintained eye contact in a way that unnerved John. *Nobody maintains eye contact with me.*

She paused again. "I should be bitter. I should hate you. I guess that deep down inside I do. But I'm more hurt than angry. When I got the telegram that said Glen was dead and I heard about you, I decided to come here. Glen would want me to devote myself to helping you. That's more productive than hating. So, here I am."

John squirmed in his chair. He looked at Marcia for reassurance. *Did I hear this woman correctly?* He couldn't decide if the strange woman was crazy or just delusional. He looked at the door and then through the window at his horse. This was not at all the greeting he had expected.

Cathy was not finished. "I found out from Marcia that you and she have a relationship similar to the one Glen and I had until he went straight. You could turn your life around and find the kind of joy Glen found."

She sounds like one of those Bible-thumping evangelists who travel from town to town. Those were the type of people John made sure he avoided.

"You and Marcia could start a new life. It would make me feel better too. I could feel that Glen didn't die for nothing." She still maintained eye contact with John. When he didn't respond, she continued. "You wouldn't even have to turn yourself in, just go somewhere and start over quietly. No one would know who—"

"The kind of joy Glen had?" John interrupted. "He's dead, lady." He got up from his chair and headed for the door. "I don't want to hear any more of this."

Marcia was on her feet in an instant, following him. Her face was red. "John, listen to me. I've been listening to Cathy a lot since she's been here. If you walk out of here now, if you turn your back on what may be the only way we can make it together, then I'll turn you in myself."

"What?" He spun around toward her.

"I'll have a deputy come out here and wait for you to come back. I'll give him the best directions I can to find your hideout. I'll do everything possible to help them catch you. Do you hear me, John Williams?" She did not let up. In fact, it seemed she didn't fear him in the least and wanted to verbally strip him of his power to bully his way through the situation.

John could hold his rage no longer. He considered taking a swing at Marcia, but instead, he grabbed the door handle and nearly it tore it off. "What makes you think I'm coming back," he said. He stepped out onto the porch and didn't wait for an answer. Ten seconds later, he had untied his horse and was in his saddle. Before Marcia could confront him again, he raced away.

⁂

Marcia could only cry great sobs. She buried her face in Cathy's shoulder as John rode out of sight.

⁂

After John's rage ebbed, he laughed at the scene at the ranch house. *Turn myself in? What a ridiculous idea. Give up this exciting life? Ha.* All his thoughts about Marcia during his journey from Colorado went up in smoke. Their relationship was definitely over—for good this time. She had given him no choice. He needed to pack his belongings at the hideout and get as far away as he could before Cathy or Marcia turned him in. He took Marcia's threat seriously.

John knew he would need to inform the gang that Herman's widow was in town and she knew their approximate location, which would make turning them into authorities quite easy. But he had no intention of telling them about his private business with Marcia.

BADMAN, Polzin

The members of the Williams Gang jumped to their feet as one. They heard a sound a short way up the trail that wound down the basin to their hideout.

Art and Al drew their guns. They spread out on either side of the trail and waited for the intruder. Lan strayed away from the trail and moved cautiously toward the approaching noise from the underbrush. The sound of horse hooves treading lightly upon the dusty, rocky ground filled the air.

"How did anyone find the entrance?" Al whispered to Art. He leaned against a stack of rocks and then spotted the intruder—it was John.

"John," Al said as he leapt from cover. "What are you doing back so soon? It's barely daylight."

"How do you know I'm not being led at gun point? I could be bringing the law down here, you idiots. You know it is possible someone might stumble upon the entrance. How can you be so careless?"

Al got the message. Things had not gone well with Marcia. He had seen this kind of tirade from John before. "Well, Lan didn't show himself."

"And what could that gunless wonder do? Maybe he could throw rocks or something."

Realizing it was pointless to defend themselves, Al and Art quietly accompanied John back to the camp at the base of the basin. John ranted and raved. Al knew he would calm down after they listened for a couple of hours.

<hr>

Not long after they returned to the lean-to, John did finally calm down. Soon after, Lan rejoined them, and the four outlaws got around to discussing future plans. They were out of money again and needed a way to come up with some if they were ever going to eat anything but rabbit stew again or enjoy themselves in any way.

"Art, you aren't known around here," Lan said. "Why don't you take the stuff we got from the railroad camp that's left and see what you can get for it?"

"Still taking the chicken way out, I see," John said. "Why not stick up the bank again?"

"We'd be running again. We wouldn't have a chance to stop for who knows how long," Lan said.

"Nobody would follow us up here," John replied.

"They might . . . now," Lan told him.

"You're hungry, aren't you, John?" Al tread gingerly.

John glared at him and then settled back. He thought about the new danger Cathy represented. It was true that they couldn't count on running back to the hideout. If Cathy and Marcia had alerted the U.S. marshal, the gang's trail would be followed. Things were worse than the others knew. The local lawmen may not wish to hunt them down, and certainly a posse made up of citizens wouldn't want to, but U.S. marshals were a different story.

Leaning his keg/chair against the lean-to wall, John considered the problem, and then he decided to tell his men about Cathy. "Craziest thing

I ever saw. I got to Marcia's, and the marshal's wife was there, waiting for me. For the record, the marshal's dead. So much for the famous Glen Herman. Billy the Kid's dead too, I hear. Pat Garrett got him. Beware the outlaw turned lawman.

"Anyway, Herman's wife wanted me to go straight, start a new life, leave you guys on your own. She tracked me down to tell me that. When I turned her down, Marcia threatened to turn me in herself. She might too. So with that threat, and the fact that a little, fragile woman can find me, we could be in for a lot more trouble than usual. So, you're right. Someone might come up here looking for us now."

Moans and disturbed looks circulated the group. For their own good, they would be thinking more as a gang from that point forward—one for all and all for one.

"I guess you're right about what we should do for now," John said, agreeing with Lan's earlier statement. Then he guffawed in his inimitable manner.

His partners shook their heads.

"Art, take the stuff to town," John said.

As Art began to gather the items to take them to town, Al contemplated his place in the group. He had grown to like Art, the increasingly sheepish and sheep-like safecracker. Art's brown hair hung in his eyes, and his stocky body never seemed to suffer from the periods of hunger the gang experienced. Al wondered what Art thought of his decision to join the group, now that he had spent the better part of two years with them.

Lan, for his part, was glad to have Art around. He was an anchor to John's steam-engine personality. Sure, Art was a disrespectful influence at times and mutinous, but Lan could live with those personality quirks more easily than John's. Lan believed that if they had a few more "specialists" like Art, they'd really have an army that would fulfill John's dream. Lan was beginning to share that dream.

John was another matter. While Lan could control John and felt a generous amount of respect for him, Lan could not like him. He was black through and through. Lan could find nothing to feel affection for, but John was the leader of what was now Lan's gang too, an enviable place to be compared to fishing in a stream without bait. Nevertheless, John's tendency to lack loyalty to his own people was always on Lan's mind.

Lan and Al had developed camaraderie. They found similarities in their backgrounds. Lan did not have a crude big brother in his childhood, but sometimes the bond between Al and Lan was more brother-like than the one between John and Al. Lan knew Al felt that way too.

John looked around at the members of his gang. He respected Lan and loved his little brother, in his own way. But Art was a thorn in John's side. However, there was something that kept Art alive, in spite of John's sentiments. Perhaps it was nothing more than John's wish to build a gang, and Art was the fourth man. He deserved some consideration for that. Art's talents could come in handy, and while John had reservations from the beginning, Art had been devout in his desire to be part of the gang from the time they met him. John liked that, and he hoped Art would eventually come around and stop rocking the boat before something had to be done about him.

Art was scared to death of John and thanked God that Lan and Al were there to control him. He'd had no idea what he was getting himself into. If he had, he wouldn't have joined the gang. But now he didn't dare try to leave. Besides, he enjoyed the power he shared as part of the Williams Gang. As long as John didn't shoot him, things would be all right. Now he was being trusted with a mission on his own, and he liked that.

While he couldn't quite take to any of the gang members as friends, he did want to belong somewhere. John was held in terrified awe by the gang, and Lan was given respect out of appreciation for his brains. Then there was Al. Art felt neither camaraderie nor animosity for Al. He was just John's younger brother and a member of the gang. Art could see no special niche for Al. He was just another gang member in Art's eyes.

That may have been a face-saving view on Art's part, nonetheless, that's how he felt.

As Art finished packing the stuff, he decided he wanted to bring back more from town than what he was sent for. He wanted to impress Lan and John and hoped that then John would ease up on him and be more sure he was worthwhile.

BADMAN, Polzin

Art rode up to the stone archway at the entrance to the hideout and dismounted. He walked his horse through the opening and started down the winding trail as rapidly as the terrain would allow. When he reached the camp at the bottom of the bowl, he relayed his news to the others.

"The whole town is buzzing. The law is rounding up a gigantic posse to come up here. A U.S. marshal, the sheriff, and some other local lawmen have sworn in a slug of deputies."

"You mean that they're actually finding people willing to come after us?" John asked. "They must have all lost their senses down there." He obviously had not expected this type of courage.

"They're pretty confident they can find us," Art said. "I hate to say it, John, but the word is that Marcia is helping the law. She's given the marshal a pretty good idea where this place is." Art cringed, knowing their hideout was about to be exposed.

"So now they figure they can trap us and that makes them feel brave," Lan said.

"I'll tell you, I was tempted not to come back," Art said. He kicked a small rock in front of him. "That would have been a lot safer for me."

"But you didn't want me looking you up after this little war is over, right?" John said as he walked over to Art and poked him in the chest. "You little coward."

"Coming back here means I took a big chance on getting killed," Art said. "I could have just walked away." It felt good, even liberating, to stand up to John.

"Not coming back would have made you a dead man."

Art shrugged. Lan gestured to Art to leave it alone.

"Well, I came back," Art said.

After a moment of thoughtful silence, John began rattling off orders and plans. "I know what we've got to do. There is no safe way now. We're going to go round up all the ammunition, food, and weapons we can lay our hands on—liquor too, while we're at it. We might as well enjoy this war. Any loose money we come across won't hurt either. We're going to be ready for them." Expecting a confrontation with the others in the gang, John drew his gun and waved it menacingly. "Any objections?"

John's knew his agitation was clear. He had been even more irritable than usual since returning from Marcia's, and the present circumstances did nothing to lessen his black mood. The looks on his gang's faces told him how they felt; to question John's decision was more unthinkable than waging war against the lawmen accumulating in town. No one even suggested running.

"Good. How much time do you figure we have?" John asked Art, putting his gun away. "How organized are they right now?"

"They're planning the big raid for a few days from now," Art said. "They need a little more time to gather all the men they think they need."

"So we can catch them off guard," John thought aloud. "They won't be prepared for us to make a raid while they're making plans." He laid out his strategy. "We'll split into two groups. Al and I will get food and ammo from the general store. You two round up some money. Hit the bank. That will mostly be a diversion, but we'll need the money later. I don't care how you two Cautious Carries do it." He aimed a stern look at Lan and Art. "Al and I will do our job, and I expect you two to do yours."

The little discussion that followed was quiet and controlled. Soon afterward, the outlaws settled down for the night. John slept fitfully. He dreamed of future battles in detail—glory-filled, triumphant detail. He never noticed that the other men were also sleeping poorly.

Art, indeed, slept poorly that night. However, his dreams did not hold the same confident results as John's.

The next morning, the sun arose only minutes before the Williams Gang. All four men took care of their daily necessities and then saddled their horses. John and Al waited for the other two to disappear over the top of the basin rim before starting out.

All the way to town, John and Al were silent. Their thoughts were secret from each other. When they reached sight of Lander, they reined in their horses and paused a little while before continuing on, making sure Art and Lan would have time to get their bank robbery underway before they hit the general store.

"I hope they make lots of noise," John said. "With those two, you never know."

Lan and Art rode quietly into Lander and tied up their horses in front of the saloon, but instead of walking into the barroom, they turned right and headed down the boardwalk, toward the bank.

A few of the passing people looked at them with curiosity, which made Lan nervous. But if anyone recognized the two members of the Williams Gang, they didn't let it show.

"I don't know why John wants us to do this," Art said.

"All that matters is that he wants a diversion so that he and Al can get the things we need from the general store," Lan replied.

"Yeah, diversion," Al said. "Decoy, you mean. He wants us to get shot at so he and Al can have smooth sailing. Well, I ain't taking no extra risks for anybody."

Lan gave him a warning look.

"Oh, we'll knock off the bank alright, but we're going to do it nice and quietly." They stood just outside the bank, contemplating their next move. "Why don't you and I just hit the bank and then high-tail it out of here on our own? What's so all-fired important about staying here to fight—for any of us? John's girl has turned against him. There's no reason for any of us to stay here."

Lan was heavily loyal to John and savored the power he held in the gang, but he saw no point in arguing with Art at this point. Lan wasn't sure what Art had in mind, but he believed it best to find out before he took any contrary action. Besides, time was wasting. The important thing was to get the bank robbery underway.

Just as the two men were about to step through the door of the bank, a ruckus began up the street, at the far end of town. People began to yell, and shots were fired. People and horses scattered in every direction.

Lan cursed. "Our timing's off. It took us too long to create a diversion."

People started streaming out of the bank. They obviously had heard the commotion down the street.

"Can it be the Williams Gang?" someone asked.

"It doesn't matter if it is," another citizen said. "We're not ready for them yet. They'll get away, like usual."

"Do we just let them help themselves to our town?" a woman said.

"Well, I ain't going to try to stop them," a gray-haired, old man replied.

"Come on, you cowards. Let's get up there," another man said. "We need to stop them now."

One by one, the crowd moved up the street at a crawling pace, urged on by the man's connotations. Even the women followed, perhaps out of curiosity or possibly pushed on by the man's persuasive appeal to make a bold step to stop the outlaws.

As the crowd pushed past Lan and Art, the outlaws moved into the bank.

"We might as well get to work on the vault," Lan said.

Lan stood at a point halfway between the door and the bank president's desk. The room was empty.

Even in the hurry to get outside to see what the commotion was down the street, someone in the bank had taken the time to close the vault. Art went to work on the combination. He cursed. "This is a tough one, but I think I can get it."

Lan heard a sound and looked up in time to see a woman descending the stairs from a mezzanine. "Alright, lady, hold it right there and nobody will get hurt."

"What will you do, shoot me with your finger?" she asked, referencing Lan's empty hands.

"I don't think you want to find out," Lan said, wondering what he actually would do to her if she called his bluff. "Don't get any ideas. I'm not alone, and the other guy has a gun. Just stay where you are."

Art emerged from behind the partition dividing the vault from the rest of the bank. He was carrying a stuffed moneybag. "Let's go," he said.

Forgetting about the woman, they went out the front door. They looked in the direction the people had gone a few minutes earlier. There was still a lot of confusion on the street, but Lan could not see any familiar figures. He started off at a trot.

"Lan, we've got the money." Art said, following Lan. "We don't have to go back to that death trap or shoot it out with the law. We could start out on our own."

Lan stopped and turned toward Art. "I don't want to hear any more of that."

Lan's face was all Art needed to see. He discarded all thoughts of continuing the argument or of setting off on his own.

But Lan wasn't through. He grabbed Art by his shirt. "Do I have to knock the tar out of you right now? We're in this together. Can I count on you? You're not going to run out on us. One way or the other, I'll see to that personally, if I have to. I may not agree with everything John says, but he's the boss, and I'd rather die as a part of this gang than have John Williams bear me a grudge and track me down. Wouldn't you?" He let go of Art.

Art stood still for a moment, considering Lan's words. His hand rested on his gun handle. Then his anger subsided. "I joined this gang voluntarily, and I sure wouldn't want John on my tail. What kind of life would it be, always worrying about not waking up because he'd gotten his kicks out of bumping me off while I was asleep?"

Lan turned and continued walking. "Well, here's some excitement for you," Lan said as they approached their horses and the crowd at the end of the street. Lan looked around, obviously considering the circumstances and deliberating about what to do next. "John and Al are going to have to make it on their own after all. Come on, let's get out of here—and distract the crowd while we're at it." Lan grinned and jumped on his horse.

John and Al stood in front of the store, helping themselves to the feed and grain bins. Occasionally, one of them would fire his gun, but nobody returned fire. The storekeeper and everybody else had taken cover. The gunfire was to discourage anyone from becoming foolishly brave.

While Al continued to lay down covering fire, John threw two bags of oats across his horse and tied them down. When he finished, they reloaded their six-shooters, mounted their horses, and bolted down the street, yelling, whooping, and shooting.

Some of the townspeople began to gather their wits and react. Perhaps because they recognized John Williams, they failed to respond with gunfire. Mostly, they stood and watched as the Williams brothers rode off. Al fired aimlessly into the air. John aimed indiscriminately at people in the crowd.

One man, obviously urging the crowd to take action, waved his arms, trying to evoke an effective response from the people around him. John aimed at the man and fired, but he missed. The man scampered away.

John and Al had loaded their horses with boxes of ammunition, extra guns, and a considerable amount of food, including the sacks of grain. As they rode through the crowd, Al thought he saw the glint of a badge. Thankfully, gunfire broke out at the other end of town, which caused many people in the crowd to focus their attention in that direction, giving John and Al the diversion they needed.

Near the bank, Lan's last-minute inspiration to draw attention away from the other outlaws played out in front of the woman who had come down the stairs in the bank. Admiringly, she watched the escape as the advancing crowd, no longer dazed, rained bullets in the direction of the outlaws. But they were too far away at that point.

It didn't take long for the Williams Gang to safely reach their basin hideout. They began preparing for the coming onslaught. In the next few days, they had a few plans of their own to carry out—plans that John and Lan thought would leave them the victors when placed against the plans of the authorities in Lander.

BADMAN, Polzin

"Lan, there is something I want to tell you," John whispered with his back to Al and Art. "Come over here."

Lan and John moved to the end of the lean-to, which the gang used as a storage area.

"I'm going to tell you something I haven't told anyone else."

Lan nodded solemnly.

"There's something I want you to know," John began again. He looked around to see if the others were far enough out of hearing range.

"Lan, I respect you. I respect you, and I trust you." John fidgeted with his hat. "I know there's a chance some or all of us might not be alive in a few days . . ."

"Well, John, I—"

"Don't interrupt. You know as well as I do, maybe better, that our position is not that great. This could be our deaths."

"Yeah, but I've got some ideas—"

"Ideas, ideas . . . will you shut up for a minute?" John was careful to keep his voice low enough that the others couldn't overhear.

"Lan, what I'm trying to tell you is that if I don't make it and you do . . . and Al does . . . I want you to look after my little brother."

Lan started to speak again, but John stopped him with a motion of his hand.

"Lan, I got him into this. I got us all into this. Al doesn't know any better. He just follows his big brother. Art . . . well, I don't know why he stayed." John stopped and looked hard at Lan. Even if he knew, he obviously wasn't going to betray Art's trust.

"But since we're in this," John continued, "I want to show those lawmen we are strong. I want to show them we are determined. This is the start of that big gang I always dreamed about. My dream will disappear if we run now. We've got to make it now or die. But if just some of us make it, I want to be sure Al will be alright. Chances are pretty good that Al won't make it on his own. I just want to make sure you understand, in case he needs help if I'm not around."

Lan opened his mouth again, and again John put up his hand.

"The secret I'm trying to tell you is about what happens if my dream fizzles." He paused and looked around. Then he turned his back to the others and put his hand by his chest so they couldn't see what he was about to do.

John pointed to a pile of loose rocks stacked a few feet high, about halfway up the side of the rock bowl. "We're not as broke as I make out," he confessed. "In that stack of rocks, there is probably fifty thousand dollars' worth of gold, silver, paper money—you name it. Everything is buried under those rocks at different levels. When I first found this place, that spot was a depression. Each time I tucked a little loot away, I added a layer of rocks. I've been doing it for years. Al never noticed. I was worried he would notice the pile growing, but he never did. "

"But you could have told Al—"

John shushed him.

Lan stood there, looking off into the distance at the pile of rocks. His mouth was open, as if he were about to speak again. Then he suddenly turned back toward John. "I have an idea. If we took some of that loot out, we could put it to work. We could make our position much stronger."

"What do you mean?"

"Al and Art won't have to know anything about the loot."

John moved his head backward slightly. *Perhaps I shared my secret with the wrong person.*

"I can sneak out of here at night," Lan continued. "If you'll help me dig up some of the stuff, I'll use it to buy us some firepower, some manpower, an army." Lan's eyes glowed as they hadn't for days.

The idea sank into John's head, but then he frowned. "Where are you going to get this stuff? How are you going to get anyone to join up with us? Even the other outlaws hate me." John rested against the lean-to. He felt a little vulnerable and knew he might be showing a side Lan had not seen before.

"I can get guys to join up with me. I know quite a few guys who would do anything for some of the kind of loot we'll be talking about."

John gave Lan a doubtful look.

"I'll demand and guarantee their loyalty to you. They'll join for the chance to be a part of our future."

"But what kind of fools would put themselves into this kind of trap?" John was skeptical, but he trusted Lan's motives.

"With the men and weapons we'll have, it won't be a trap. If the law gets wind of what we're doing, there might not even be a raid." Lan scratched his chin. "It'll be a chance for revenge against all the things the law has done to these guys. There are already four fools here. Why is it so hard to see a few more?"

John still was not unconvinced.

"Don't you trust me? You just said you did."

"Of course I trust you. I wouldn't have told you about the loot otherwise. It's just that I hate to part with any of the riches."

"Which is better, rich and dead or semi-rich and feared throughout the West? We'll get some fancy weapons—some heavy firepower with the money. We'll be in great shape and be the ones in control. Let them try to get us. We know this terrain better than they do. We know all the nooks and crannies, which means we know where to hide. We can pick them off one by one before they even have a chance to make a real advance against us . . . what do you say?"

John thought for a minute, looking around, taking everything in. *Lan has a point. In fact, he made several good points.* "Alright, let's do it."

After dark, while the other outlaws were asleep, Lan and John snuck away and went to the rock pile.

"The first loot we should run across should be right on top here," John said, pointing. "I put it there just before we left Wyoming." John moved a few rocks aside and pulled out a wad of money. "Think that'll be enough?"

Lan took the money from John and rippled through it. "Yeah, this ought to do just fine."

John helped Lan pile the rocks back on the stack and then walked back to the lean-to, where Art and Al still slept soundly. Then John and Lan curled up in their blankets and drifted off for a few hours of sleep.

Twenty-four nervous hours later, John barely saw Lan start down the windy trail. He was followed by three other men and their horses.

When they reached the bottom of the bowl, Lan approached the leader of the gang. "John, I've got some good men here," Lan said. "This is Ron Stone and Steve Perkins." He gestured first at the shaggy-haired man with thick, bushy eyebrows and then to a tough-looking but clean-cut, taller man. Lan put his hand on the third new man's shoulder. "And this guy here is Gary Beethoven. He has a college education, or at least part of one. He'll be a great help in setting up this little war of ours."

John looked over the new members of his gang. The first two looked OK to him. He could handle them. But Beethoven seemed like he might need an eye kept on him. John looked at Lan. "This is all the army you could bring back?"

"Well, there's one more up at the top of the rim. His name is Les Brass. Gary suggested a sentry. We need to set up some defenses on the outside of the bowl. If anybody gets in here, it's already too late."

"Beethoven came up with that?"

Lan just shrugged.

☙ ❧

Al and Art were awakened by the movement in the hideout. For a few minutes, they watched curiously from afar.

"What is John up to now?" Art asked.

Al shook his head. "There is only one way to find out." He led the way toward the growing group of men

"Who are the newcomers?" Al asked.

"Our saviors, Al," Lan said. "With their help, we'll fight our way out of this jam and maybe take total control of this part of Wyoming."

"Alright!" Al cheered. It was the first time he'd felt like cheering since they had decided to fight it out from the rock-walled hideout.

☙ ❧

"Lan, I want to talk to you a minute." John walked away from the group, and Lan followed.

"You guys get acquainted," Lan said over his shoulder. "Gary, tell them some of your ideas."

When they had gotten beyond the earshot of the others, John turned toward Lan. "What are you trying to do? We don't need a college man— especially one who thinks he is smarter than we are—trying to tell us what to do."

"I've gone all through the leadership bit with him already. These guys know who's in charge. Ron's got the brains of a flea; he's no threat. You give Steve some little prize, and he'll be loyal forever. I sprung him from a hanging party. So, what are you worried about?"

"You sprang one of those guys from a hangin' party? What were they hangin' him for?"

"He burned down some buildings on a ranch. Strictly professional, he was paid to do it. He's not nuts."

John paused, digested that, and then went on. "Yeah, well. It's that

Beethoven guy who worries me. There's something funny about his name too."

"He's no relation to the composer . . ."

"What?"

"He's alright, John. I know you; you're afraid his brains will challenge your leadership, but I'll vouch for him. He wants to be a part of something big like this. He wants us, and we need him." Lan looked away from John for a second. "He's an outlaw, just like us."

"We don't need no more brains. You and me have enough."

"John, I don't know how to say this . . . but I really think we should make him third in command."

"Al is—"

"I knew you'd react this way, but think about it. Do you think Al could hold this gang together in our absence?"

John rubbed his forehead and sighed. "Probably not." He was quiet for a minute.

"Gary has some ideas that go beyond our defense of this place. He's got ideas of us becoming the law around here."

"We're not turning into lawmen," John said, thinking of Glen Herman.

"He means setting up our own laws and running things. It's happened other places. We'd take over the surrounding area and appoint our own sheriff and deputies. We'd collect taxes to keep our pockets full. We wouldn't have to take any risks."

John didn't like the vision Lan was painting. *Did I make the wrong choice appointing Lan as my successor? Or is Lan on to something? Having a continual revenue stream without taking any risks is appealing, but what about the excitement?*

"Come on, John. Let's get started planning."

John relaxed and smiled. "It might just work. And now all of these guys are committed to us since they know their way up here. If they try to leave, I'll shoot them." John let out one of his familiar laughs. This time, it left Lan smiling.

The two kingpins of the Williams Gang went to rejoin the others. As they walked around the kegs the others were sitting on, inside one of the lean-tos, John asked, "Well, how are you guys doing? Getting to know each other?"

"We were just about to set up a poker game," Art said. "Steve here has some cards. Want to get in?"

"Why not?" John said. "Lan?"

"No, thanks. I'll just watch."

The men spread the cards out, inspected them, and then allowed Steve to deal the first hand. Hard coin was the only accepted wagering material.

Hours later, as the game wound down, Gary Beethoven sat with a stack of money in front of him.

"Well, I think I'll turn in," Lan said.

"Yeah, me too," Al said.

One by one, the others begged off and sought out a place to lay their bedrolls.

"You're not quitting, Beethoven," John said. "I want to win back some of that money."

"I'm getting tired. Maybe another time." Gary stood up.

"Sit down," John said. He drew his gun.

"John, cut it out. There'll be lots of poker games and lots more money, if we don't kill each other." Lan stepped between John and Gary.

John could see that his gun wasn't going to bluff Lan out of the way. John thought for a minute and then holstered his gun. He turned away. "You play a mighty lucky brand of poker, college boy." He turned back and spit at Gary's feet, just missing them.

"All a matter of odds," Gary said. "Not luck."

John glared at him. He had been right about this one—he thought he was better than everybody else.

⚜

Gary looked to Lan, questioning what had just happened.

Lan could only shrug as an answer.

⚜

The next morning, the men gathered around the newly lit fire, drinking their coffee, trying to get their eyes open.

Gary was the first to speak. "First, after we lay this all out, I'll send Les out to bring back some young kids I've already got picked out. They're feisty kids, you know, the kind who think they're hot stuff."

John stared at Gary. *I probably should just shoot him now. Who does he think he is to be giving orders and sending others out on errands?*

"They're our first line of defense—our infantry." Gary smiled in John's direction and then looked toward Lan. "By the way, you haven't met Les yet, John. Just remember, he's stubby and he's jolly most of the time. But he can get very, very mean. He likes to cook, and that'll come in handy if we're holed up here very long. But don't any of you make any remarks about cooking not being masculine . . . understand?" He looked each man in the eyes, obviously wanting to make sure they understood his warning.

"Who do you think you are giving orders to?" John felt his face turning red.

Lan stepped between the two belligerents. "He's just suggesting, informing."

"It sounds more like orders to me."

"I didn't mean to rile you." Gary looked from John to Lan. The look said Gary didn't know how to cope with John's touchiness. "Alright," he continued, "up on the rimrocks, we've got a Gatling gun."

"A what?" John asked.

Everyone but Lan had his mouth open.

"A Gatling gun," Gary said. He turned toward Steve and Ron. "That's what we were pulling behind us, under the canvas on that wagon we left up there with Les."

"Where'd you get one of those?" John asked.

"I got it. That's all that matters." Gary continued with his plans. "We're going to move it away from the archway to draw attention away from the entrance. I looked around before you guys were up and spotted some flat places in the rocks, on the outside of the rim, that are well protected but give a good view of the surrounding area. We'll have a twenty-four-hour guard stationed at each of those spots and one stationed with the gun. That's both now and after this war is over."

John didn't like the way this conversation was going. Gary had some good ideas, and he certainly seemed to want to win this war, but this type of leadership might cause the others to begin to question John's leadership. He stood up. "Lan and Gary, I want to talk to you privately — the rest of you finish up your breakfast."

John put his hand on the other two men's backs, nearly pushing them inside one of the other lean-tos. He was not happy.

Lan must have sensed John's feelings because he spoke up first. "Gary's idea is that the rest of the new guys will never be inside the hideout. The less they know the better. We want to make sure they know their place. They don't come inside, they just take orders, and they get one-eighth of the take from our operations."

"One-eighth of the take?" John said. "Says who?"

"I negotiated the terms," Lan said.

John sat down.

Gary explained, "Each of the lookouts will have a couple of rifles and six-guns. There will also be a case of ammunition for each post. And before you ask, we brought that much ammunition on the wagon with the Gatling gun."

John wondered how Gary had come up with such an elaborate plan in such a short period of time.

"Les has been unloading the wagon and spreading the arsenal among the lookout positions while we've been talking," Gary said. "We'll have a message system set up so the boys can communicate with each other and us from the lookouts. I think maybe we could use Les and Art here, as sergeants of the guards. They can periodically check how things are going. They can bring the men all the food they need, as well as other supplies, so that they will not need to leave their posts. While we're under siege, they'll sleep in shifts at their positions, if things let up enough to allow sleep."

With each new bit of information, John could feel his leadership slipping away. He couldn't argue with this plan, but he was not going to give up his gang. He would die first.

"After this war is over, the men will spend their off time however they want," Gary said. "Of course, they'll still be in our army. Later, some of them may take influential positions in town as our sheriff, mayor, and such."

"Wait a minute. I don't like the way this guy is setting up sheriffs and mayors and stuff." John looked at Lan. "Who's in charge here?"

"You are, of course, John. Just think of how you set up that raid on the town." Lan smiled.

John smiled back as he remembered the excitement of the raid. "Go ahead, Gary."

"Well, for now, that's about it. After the battle, we'll work out the permanent details." He turned to go. "I'll go up and send Les on his way to round up the kids."

"You sound pretty confident about the way this war is going to turn out," John said.

"I am," Gary said. "The law and the military always think in a straight line. They're pretty easy to outsmart. I know how they think."

"One more question," John said. Gary turned toward him. "With these young troops we're adding, how many will we have?"

Lan answered for Gary. "Thirty-seven." Lan grinned.

BADMAN, Polzin

The Williams Gang spent the next week making additional preparations. Still, the awaited attack did not come.

In town, the unnoticed members of the Williams Gang's lower echelons heard only that there would be an upcoming attack. No one seemed to know when it was going to happen. There was a little talk about the possibility of involving the U.S. Cavalry, but direct involvement did not seem likely. When the news was carried back to the hideout, however, it did cause a stir.

"The cavalry?" Gary gasped. *How will we withstand an attack from the cavalry? We don't have enough men, ammunition, or supplies.*

"He just said there was talk about it," Lan said. "No one seems to think it's likely."

"So, what if the Cavalry's in on it?" John said. "That's what I've always wanted. We've got the gang to take on the U.S. Cavalry."

"We don't have near enough fire power to take on the army," Gary said. "Maybe someday we'll fulfill your dream, but this is not the time."

"If the cavalry does get involved, we won't have much choice in the matter," Lan said. "We've got to do what we can to prepare for that possibility."

Gary went out to the rest of the gang and filled them in on the details of their strategy.

Another week passed. The various members of the gang tended to their usual tasks. No one in the gang had expected to have so much time to prepare for the eventual attack. Some of them even began to doubt that it would happen.

With all the food they could foresee needing stashed around the shanties at the hideout and all the firepower and support supplies needed for a prolonged battle, John, Lan, Al, and Gary believed they were as ready as they ever would be, even though they still felt the odds had to be against them.

Lan sent Les, Steve, and Ron out to scrounge outlying towns for last minute contingent supplies. To Les' surprise, the town of Wind River, which was first on their list of possible sources for their needs, was a good choice.

"Whoo-hoo," Les said at this fortuitous choice of towns. "There's a bank, a livery stable, a feed store, a general store, and two saloons."

"Not to mention a church," one of the gang's kids said, "and lots of other stuff."

"The church won't do them no good," Les said, "us either."

The men scattered via a prearranged plan and covered the town from end to end. The outlaws stole horses, clothing, tack, money, ammunition, and everything else they wanted, whether it would be useful in their battle or not.

They loaded their wagon with virtually no interference from the locals, who were stunned by what was happening.

"Should we take a captive?" one young gun asked Les.

Les shook his head. "What for? That's John's thing, and it only leads to trouble for us—more trouble than usual, that is."

Only slightly cowed, the young outlaw became defensive. "I was just thinking . . . I ain't never had a woman."

"We only take what we can carry and then get back to the hideout."

Les altered their plan to raid several towns since the first one had fully stocked their needs. The wagon couldn't carry anything else.

The raiding party returned to the hideout by the same meandering path used to reach its destination.

Two days later, Lan's sub-party also returned to the hideout. His group was hauling a large wagon behind a team of horses.

After reporting to John, Lan, Gary, and the other leaders, Les dispatched orders to the young men of their infantry. Les unloaded some of the items from the wagon and then had one of the other young men pull the wagon to a depression among some boulders that were outside the rimrocks.

The return of the men came just in time. Less than twenty-four hours later, in the late fall afternoon, one of the sentries saw a cloud of dust in the distance and sent a message down to the leaders.

In a few minutes, more of the guards could see the riders. They guessed that there were a hundred of them. Apparently, central Wyoming had finally gotten fed up with the Williams Gang and decided it was time to do battle with them. The fact that new snow would begin to fall in a month, giving the gang added protection, probably had forced the lawmen's decision.

Motion rippled through the camp. Since the young men had been brought in, apprehension had been high. Now, the moment was indeed here. It was obvious the lawmen had good information on the location of the hideout. Whether it was from Marcia or from some other source, it didn't matter.

Art and Les went around the circle of the rimrocks, in opposite directions, meshing the actions of the Williams Gang. The posse would be allowed in range before the sentry positions would be given away. Then, the war would begin.

With the anticipated lack of imagination, the lawmen approached directly from town, in double file. Presumably, they would split the search for their foes and a way into the basin.

The posse reached the rocky climb to the archway and split into three groups. One group veered to the left. One group turned to the right. The third group, headed by the sheriff himself, continued straight up the hill.

At the time of the split, one of the lookouts gave the signal to begin firing. The Gatling gun erupted, mowing down men and horses who were running toward its secret position. Rifle fire echoed among the rocks, and the lawmen dove for cover. They were caught in the crossfire from all directions.

Nearly half of the posse fell in the initial flurry of action. The lawmen who survived took cover behind small boulders and began to fire back. But they couldn't even see the outlaws, who remained safely entrenched in their secure hiding places. The best the lawmen could do for targets was pay attention to the bursts of smoke, the accompanying sound from the rifle shots, and the growl of the big gun.

Once the little existing cover for the lawmen was exploited and the surprise of their violent reception passed, the fighting settled down to tedious pot shots. In effect, the posse was in siege, even though they were the invaders.

⚜

John's order was passed along to the men with the Gatling gun to save the ammunition for when its firepower could best be put to use. Once the posse scattered, the gun's effectiveness fell off. John gave the order to conserve rifle ammo also.

Gary, Lan, and John knew this would be a prolonged battle, requiring strategy beyond that of the surprise ambush. There was no sense wasting shots trying to hit hidden targets.

While the sporadic fighting continued along the rimrocks, seven of the gang's leaders relaxed inside a lean-to on the inside of the bowl. They were confident as they planned the next necessary moves.

Les was relieved of his sergeant-of-the-guard duties by Steve, who was told to report any important changes in the battle.

"I figure the sheriff will try to sneak a few men closer to our gun positions as soon as he thinks he can get away with it," Gary said as he joined John and Lan, who had moved off by themselves. "If he's unsuccessful, and I'm sure he will be since the approach to each position is visible from the next, he'll probably wait until dark. After dark, he may try an all-out charge, or he may try infiltration again."

"So what do we do?" John asked.

"While we're waiting for their first attempts to reach our gun positions, I think we'd better get Les busy preparing meals," Gary said. "The boys will be hungry by the time the shooting dies down a little more. We'll make a thorough check on ammo and supplies, make sure our manpower is distributed well, and see what our casualties are."

Gary popped his head out of the lean-to, making sure nobody was outside listening. Once he saw everything was all clear, he continued. "Then, we'll pull all our men into a gauntlet paralleling the archway. That's the only way in here. The rimrocks all the way around are too steep for anybody to scale. After the lawmen scout around our former positions and finding nothing but rock wall, they'll eventually gather at the archway and try to make their way in."

Lan nodded his head. "And when they start through the archway, the lawmen will be inside a little funnel we've made, and we'll mow then down."

"Wait a minute." John said. "What if they get to the archway, realize what we're up to, and don't go in?" John tapped his foot up and down.

"Then we sit back and wait them out," Gary said. "Maybe we'll have to come up with an alternate plan if that happens, but we'll have time to think about that when the time comes. We're in a very good position to wait them out, though."

"Really?" John looked skeptical. "We have limited supplies. They know that. They can wait us out because they have access to a continual flow of supplies—including food. They can always go back to town for more of what they need."

"Take it easy, John," Gary said. "The odds are much more even now. There are only a few more of them than there are of us. As far as going back to town for reinforcements, they can't get off this mound without passing through our gun sights."

John leaned back against the wall and laughed.

To Gary, that seemed like an uncharacteristic action for the circumstances. He didn't know that is was not unusual for John. *I guess he thinks I have everything covered.*

The leaders set out to do the tasks assigned to them, just as Gary specified.

On the outside of the rim, the sheriff passed the word to close in on the outlaws' firing positions. The outlaws let the lawmen's cover fire fly unreturned, until the posse's movements offered good targets.

Situated comfortably behind their protective shelters, the outlaws picked off the advancing lawmen. Eventually, the sheriff realized his men could not reach their objectives as planned, and he stopped the advance. They settled in at sundown to wait out the outlaws.

John, Lan, Gary, and Al sat around a small campfire in the darkness, finishing their meals with Steve, Art, and Ron.

"So far, things are going along as planned," Gary said. "Les has spread the word to form an opening in our lines for the attackers to use, thus trapping them between our men, who will be firing from both sides. Soon we should hear a lot of gunfire."

"This is a real war," Lan said.

Al shushed them. "I think I hear something."

"I don't hear any shots yet," John said.

Al looked into the darkness. "I think someone is inside the bowl."

"How?"

"Shhh. He might be right," Gary said. "We should be on guard here, just in case something goes wrong. They will be heading right up to the entrance . . . if any make it through."

"But we haven't heard any gunshots yet . . ." John said. He stopped as Al darted away from the group and into the darkness.

John's eyes followed Al, who was swallowed by the silent, dark night. Suddenly, there were the sounds of a skirmish nearby. Then Al came stumbling back into the ring of firelight, pushing a man along in front of him. Al shoved him to the ground, on his face, beside the campfire.

"He was trying to get a good shot at us from behind a rock, just thirty feet away," Al said. He put his knife away and handed John the man's gun.

"Not all of you, just him," the man said, looking up from the ground, pointing at John. He got up to his knees but didn't go any further. He obviously knew one of the men would attack him.

John recognized him. He was one of the rustlers from Colorado — one of the men he had presumed dead.

"You ran out on us," the man said. "You turned tail and ran . . . you coward."

John jumped to his feet. He grabbed his holstered gun, forgetting his other hand held the gun Al gave him.

Lan jumped to his feet and held John's hand in place. John glared at

Lan, but Lan held his ground. The rustler continued to talk.

"I tracked you all the way from Colorado. You told us you were from around Lander. When I got into town, a woman was telling the sheriff to round up a posse and she would help him find you. So, I joined up with the posse."

"How did you get in here?" Gary asked. "Did anyone else get in?"

In the distance, they could hear the sound of gunfire.

"I didn't follow the sheriff's orders," the man said. "I made my way up the hill by myself, right after nightfall, but before his men started moving in. It sounds like you set a trap for the sheriff. He should have done what I did. One man can get in here but not a whole posse. In the dark, your men thought I was one of them." The rustler grinned. He seemed unconcerned about his tenuous situation. "I'm here for my own reasons. All I want is you, John Williams. I found you." He glared wildly at John. "That's all I set out to do . . . just to kill you. You didn't even try to help us back in that canyon. We might have had a chance."

John pulled free of Lan's grip, grabbed the knife from inside the top of Al's boot, and turned to the intruder. "You didn't have a chance." He slit the man's throat in one quick motion—too quickly for anyone to stop.

The man feel face down in the dirt. His left hand landed in the fire, and blood pooled under his head.

The outlaws looked at each other in shock.

"Get him out of here, Art." Lan motioned at the body.

No one said anything. They watched while Art dragged the man away. John crouched belligerently, facing the others, the knife still in his hand.

The gunfire had died down outside the hideout. Gary looked up from the piece of ground he had been staring at in an attempt to wipe the gory spectacle he had just witnessed from his mind. He returned his thoughts to the battle raging around them.

"I guess our plan worked, or we'd be wallowing in lead by now," Steve said.

John spoke up. "Go get a status report, Steve. Find out how many men we lost and what the posse looks like now."

Steve did as he was told. The others watched Steve trot up the winding trail to the rimrocks until he vanished in the black night. The remaining leaders formed a loose circle around the fire. John moved away from the others. Everybody was lost in thought as the reality of the situation sunk in.

⁂

Hours passed, and nobody spoke. Curiosity began to get the best of them as they awaited Steve's return. Art was about to voice his concern regarding Steve's tardiness when he finally showed his face again.

He approached the group, smiled, and gave his report. "We've only lost two men. One fool stood up and—"

Gary interrupted Steve's report. "Just the important facts, Steve. Time may be important."

"Well, subtracting the bodies we could see, from how many lawmen we figure were left before sundown, there can't be more than twenty of them now."

"How did any get away?" Lan asked.

"When the first few got to the end of the gauntlet, some of the others weren't into the trap yet. The boys couldn't fire at them without taking a chance of hitting some of our own men. And they couldn't have waited any longer or some of the lawmen would have gotten through. When the boys started firing at the lead group, some of the lawmen retreated and got away."

"What do we do now?" Al asked.

"We wait," Gary said. "Right now, I'd say we are in a stage of siege."

"What if they use the darkness to send for more supplies or reinforcements?" John asked.

"I think if they leave now, they won't come back," Gary said. "I think the heavy losses will kill the desire of anyone from town who isn't a lawman. Once the runners get out of here, I don't think they will come back. Whether I'm wrong or right, we just sit here until we aren't able to wait any longer. What other choice is there?"

Nobody offered any other alternatives.

"Art, Ron, go help make our soldiers comfortable. This could be a long siege, possibly weeks. Snow is only a little ways off. We could still be here like this when it comes. Better make plans for shelters up there in the rocks. Give the boys an idea about what's going on, and a little pep talk wouldn't hurt."

Art and Ron left the warm fire to climb slowly up the circular trail to the rimrocks. When they reached the top, they looked out and spotted little fires glowing behind the boulder hiding places of the posse. It was evident that the sheriff had indeed decided to wait out the outlaws.

Morning came, and the sheriff had to admit to himself that they were unprepared for a long siege. He had fully expected to overrun the hideout but was forced to change his plans. His men were hungry, and their ammunition was low. The discovery of the Gatling gun and total firepower of the outlaws was stunning. The sheriff had no choice but to lay siege to the hideout if he wanted a successful outcome to his campaign against the Williams Gang.

Two deputies were chosen to return to town for food and ammunition. Three others were told to search out reinforcements, possibly from the U.S. Cavalry detachment at Fort Laramie—the one they had spoken with earlier. There was a movement to make Wyoming a state. The outlaw element would have to be dealt with, if congress were to be convinced of the feasibility of such a thing. So, the cavalry might possibly be persuaded to join the fight.

The five chosen deputies rose from their conference with the sheriff and mounted their horses. Just as they reached the inside of the range, the Gatling gun roared to life, mowing down all five men and their horses.

The Williams Gang's gunners cheered while the sheriff cursed his thoughtlessness and decided to try again after another sunset. His thoughts began to drift from victory to survival. He silently mourned the men who died as a result of his smugness.

Once again, outguessing the law, Gary ordered his men to move the Gatling gun down the hill under the cover of darkness. They set it up at the base of the rocks, near the remaining members of the posse.

The cluster of lawmen felt safe. The sheriff was baffled by the noises he heard the outlaws making, but he was confident in his posse and his newly formed plan. He dispatched two more deputies to secure supplies, this time telling them to take a route beyond the Gatling gun's ability to reach them.

As soon as the sounds of trotting horses filled the air, the Gatling gun opened fire. The unexpected shots wiped out the messengers and startled the rest of the posse. They were confused by the new position of the gun, and panic spread throughout their camp. The men flew in all directions.

As the men scrambled for their lives on horseback or on foot, the riflemen on the rimrocks held their fire. The sheriff assumed they were unable to see well enough to shoot effectively. Still, the Gatling gun roared on, but it received only a lonely reply of spaced out gunfire from the fleeing posse. With the aid of the darkness, fifteen of the original force of lawmen escaped. The sheriff, determined to return in victory and vengeance, was among them.

The battle was over. The outlaws had won. But the war was not over.

The next morning, John awakened his brother. "Al," he said, "we just had a big victory. We came through a scary battle. It got me to thinking."

"Did you have to wake me up so early? I'm still tired." Al yawned.

"Listen up, little brother. I need to talk to you before the others get moving." John stepped outside the lean-to. "Come here. Let's take a walk."

Al threw off his blanket and shuffled after his brother. When they were out of earshot of the rest of the gang, John told Al what was on his mind. "Al, you know how much you mean to me. We've been all each other's had since we were kids. I look out for you, and you look up to me . . . at least you used to."

"I still do."

"Yeah, well . . . I wonder if you think less of me because I let Lan have so much say in what goes on in our gang. I mean, I let him give you orders. Now, Beethoven gives you, and sometimes me, orders. I think maybe you're wondering what happened to your place with your big brother."

"I'm not a leader, especially a leader of men like these." Al motioned toward the sleepers.

"That's right. I'm looking out for the good of the gang and for you. This is my dream. Lan takes care of things . . . and as long as Lan keeps him in line, that Beethoven guy can help us too."

"I know." Al nodded.

"But you don't have to take any gruff from anybody. You're still my little brother."

"Well, sometimes it seems more like Lan's your brother, and I'm just another member of the gang . . ."

"You're the most important thing to me—even more important than my dream, and I won't let anybody, or anything, come between us."

Al looked down at the ground, considering his response, and they slowed their pace. "Then let's give up this dream of yours. Can't we just be two brothers, instead of two outlaw brothers?"

"Too late for that. Besides, our dream is too important. I can make things good for you and my gang. That's what I want."

"Right. I'm the most important thing to you . . . right after the gang."

"I may look after you, but I'm not above knocking you down a peg if you press me." John clenched his teeth.

Al frowned. "Can I go back to sleep now?" He knew resistance was futile.

John watched Al return to the lean-to with mixed emotions. He wanted to please his little brother, but Al just didn't understand his big brother's needs. Al was the most important thing in John's life. But why couldn't Al take more pleasure in the exciting life they were leading?

John kicked at a stone and decided to wander up the trail. He noticed for the first time that it was pretty chilly for that time of day.

A few days after the unsuccessful siege on the hideout, the gang took inventory of their forces and supplies.

"We've still got enough ammunition left, and our manpower is good," Gary said. "Most importantly, enthusiasm among the troops is high. We have the best possible set of circumstances to take over Lander. We're in good shape, and the law is not. Our reports say no one in town is willing to serve on a posse, and the sheriff is unable to get the cavalry. Lander is ours for the taking."

The leaders of the Williams Gang sat around the morning campfire. The air was cold, and their breath puffed out of their mouths in little clouds. Occasional flakes of snow fluttered to the ground. They finished off the last of the coffee and piled their plates and eating utensils in the barrel sink.

"When the day warms up a little, we'll take all but a dozen of the men and head for town," Gary said. "Les stays here to take care of the boys who stay back. We'll be gone for a while. They'll need him to take care of their needs. Of course, you'll need to look out for our interests as well, Les." He turned to the jolly cook. "Don't let anyone else into the bowl."

Les shrugged. He had hoped for a bed in town. But he would take what he could get. He turned and headed up the trail toward the rimrocks to pick out the men who would stay behind. That was his privilege as the one in charge of the young members of their gang.

He soon sent the men who were going to town to fetch their horses from the concealed corral about a mile from the base of the mound. John, Lan, Gary, Al, Art, Steve, and Ron were going to meet them in an hour to start the trek to Lander.

Even via their winding route, chosen to encircle town, the trip took very little time. The outlaws then split into two groups and approached Lander from opposite ends. Lan led one group of men, and John, with Al at his side, led the other.

Midday congestion was nonexistent as John, Al, and four of the young men headed for the mayor's office. The official was sitting calmly behind his desk when John and Al walked in. The others had been left outside to tend to anyone who might want to interfere.

"Mr. Mayor," John said with false reverence, "we're taking over the town. I don't even care what you think about it. Some of my men are over at the marshal's office. Some are at the telegraph office, others are with the sheriff, and everyone else of importance is here." John smirked as he jerked the mayor from his chair and pushed him toward the door. "As of this moment, you're no longer in office, and this town is run by the Williams Gang."

They reached the street, and John gave the mayor one last shove. Then John drew his gun and fired a bullet into the mayor's heart.

"John," Al said. His plea was too late.

"We didn't need him around, stirring up trouble for us. Those big shots can't ever quit being big shots. He would have been in the way . . . besides, now we're less likely to get any resistance from anybody else. They'll know what to expect." John cocked his head back in his ritualistic laughter. "That felt good!"

Meanwhile, only a short distance down the street, Gary was handling the sheriff in a slightly different way.

"Sheriff, you blew your only chance to stop this gang," Gary said. "Now, I hope you're not going to make it necessary for me to kill you. We'll have our own sheriff from now on, but you can keep on being a human being if you want to . . . that means, keep living, if you don't make trouble and behave yourself."

Lan shoved the sheriff to his knees in the street, while Gary covered him with his gun. The other gang members were herding the townspeople toward them.

"I want you to tell these people how smart it will be for them to go along with our plans and not resist," Gary continued.

"Right now," Lan added as he kicked the sheriff in the back.

"I'm afraid they have us under their control," the sheriff said. "It would be safer if you didn't resist, until we can organize . . ."

Lan gave the sheriff another sharp kick in his back.

"No glory seeking, Sheriff, I mean, ex-sheriff," Gary said. Then he addressed the people. "As soon as the excitement dies down, you'll be free to go about your business. Your guns and ammunition are being rounded up, along with any other weapons. If you need them for any reason, they can be checked out from your new sheriff, Steve Perkins. All of you folks will find that life won't be much different under our rule. There'll be a few changes, but if you don't do anything stupid, you'll be alright."

Gary made eye contact with as many of the townspeople as he could, and he saw fear in their eyes. He had them right where he wanted them. "No one will be allowed to leave town without one of our men going along. There will be sentries set up all around this place, with orders to 'shoot to kill' anyone moving at night or not checking with the proper authorities."

Lan took up the oratory. "As the man said, your weapons will be kept by the sheriff—the new sheriff—and checked out only as he sees fit. There will be no telegraph in town. The wires are being dismantled outside town right now. If anyone outside wants to know why, they'll be told our town wants to be left alone."

"Your men are already plundering our homes and businesses," one man in the crowd said. "We won't sit back and take that kind of thing."

"That sort of thing is bound to happen," John said as he joined them. He laughed, drew his gun, and shot the man who had protested. "Anybody else got any complaints?" John looked around, and no one spoke up. He signaled for Lan and Gary to continue.

"The boys will tire of plundering soon, and then things will be back to normal," Gary said.

"Yeah, when everything they hanker for is gone, they'll stop plundering," John added and let out a whoop.

"All we're going to ask of you is cooperation, since you won't give us your respect," Gary continued. "You really don't have a choice. You'll share your prosperity with us . . . sort of a tax to stay alive."

"Hey, that's the sheriff." John motioned toward the man now

kneeling on the ground. "Why is he still alive?"

"He's going to be our first guest in his old jail," Lan said. He really was just hoping to avoid another cold-blooded killing.

"Yeah, that sounds alright. Give him a taste of how the other half lives, before he dies." John laughed again.

"Maybe we should do what they say," another town leader said. "We don't need any more killings."

Gary drowned out the town's murmured acceptance. "Alright. You can start getting back to your lives. Let what you know about the Williams Gang, and what you saw here, remind you to avoid trouble."

The crowd dispersed. The citizens of Lander returned to their stores and homes, trying to figure out how to adjust to this new life without being shot.

The townspeople were just hoping to live in freedom, which is why they chose the wilderness of Wyoming in the first place. Instead, they found themselves effectively cut off from the outside. A few miles in each direction around Lander was their world. But little by little, they learned to tolerate the outlaws' control of them.

Strangers were met outside of town, and in what seemed to be chance encounters, they were escorted throughout their visits. One of the fledgling outlaws would tag along with the newcomers like a good-natured youngster and make sure none of the townspeople told the strangers about what was going on in Lander. Sometimes the gang had to convince the curious outsiders that friends or relatives had passed through and were no longer there. And sometimes, other means of keeping tabs on people who entered the area were necessary. But always, the outlaws knew what the strangers were being told and what they were saying.

"Talkers seldom got a second chance," one stranger, who came to stay, commented to others in the saloon. "Once we knew what was going on, we weren't allowed to leave. Like those who made comments about how word was getting around that a young boy, or someone, seemed to meet everyone who came to town. Then there were those who moved to Lander intentionally, not knowing what they were getting into. There were also those who came looking for someone who had disappeared and also became residents. They were given an ultimatum . . . stay peacefully or be killed."

The governmental system that the outlaws installed in central Wyoming did not include John Williams. He stayed outside the system and observed.

"Interesting election, eh, Gary?" John said shortly after the gang had taken over. "Probably the only time the mayor has been elected unanimously."

Gary chuckled from the mayor's chair and looked out the window. "And unlike the last mayor, I don't need another job to support myself." He laughed.

"I think I'll wander over and see how Sheriff Perkins is doing."

"Oh, he's over at the marshal's office, visiting Les."

John shook his head. "I'm not sure it was a good idea making Les the marshal."

"Oh, Steve takes care of all the real enforcement. All the fuss between townsfolk is taken care of by the sheriff's office. The only time Les gets involved in anything is when someone takes on the gang. Then, it's no time for hard decisions. By your order, it's shoot first, and ask no questions."

"It's a great policy, I think. Well, I'll see ya." John stepped out into the cold daylight and found small snowflakes drifting earthward. It was November. A year had passed with the gang in control of the town. The weather made John think of rougher times. Then he smiled. The gang's organization in town fulfilled his dream. The leaders now only used the hideout as a secret retreat. Some of the gang members found housing in the former homes of ousted residents who had to fend for themselves. Even Les finally got his comfortable bed in town when he convinced

Lan and John to let him be the marshal. Some of the young outlaws even moved in with families—mostly families with attractive, young daughters.

John set up his headquarters in two rooms of the hotel. Some of the other outlaws took rooms there as well. With the town being closed, there wasn't any other use for hotel space, so John shut it down to the public.

With the law enforcement around Lander at an all-time low in ability to resist because they were pressed to handle the range wars and Indian uprisings, the Williams Gang was the sole controlling force. And the town pretty well ran itself, allowing the mayor to spend his time acting as bookkeeper and accountant for the gang. He helped all the gang's moneymaking and law enforcement segments run smoothly and work together. He also assisted John in planning his carousing in neighboring towns. The mayor didn't want his own town ruined.

Colorado was in the process of gaining its statehood, with civilized society holding reign over the frontier life, but Wyoming still had its share of troubles. The situation in Lander, though certainly known, was overlooked. The statehood element was pushing for some sort of cleanup campaign, and all the while, the open range ranchers were feeling more and more cooped in by the barbed-wire fences springing up around them. The other problems like sheep men battling cattlemen and the corruption of the Campbell group in the capital made the Williams Gang unimportant, except perhaps to the people of Lander.

One wintry night, the forgotten sheriff sat in his cell behind the office he used to call his own, waiting for the fate he was only too sure would be a bullet from John Williams's gun, whenever it came. He listened to the howling wind outside.

"Sheriff Swift . . . Jerry, are you in there?" a voice outside his window said.

"Of course I'm here. Who is that?" the former sheriff quietly responded.

"It's Will Cather. Are you alone?"

"Yeah, I don't know where Perkins is. He left a while ago. Why?"

"Me and some other boys are here to get you out. You're our only hope for getting us out of this mess."

A rope flew into the cold cell through the barred window. The sheriff, who normally avoided the cold area of the cell near the window, wrapped the loose end of the rope tightly around the bars and returned it to his rescuers. There was a momentary silence, then grunting, and then clopping hooves as a horse was coerced into straining against the solidity of the cement holding the bars in place. Suddenly, the bars yanked free of the wall, amid cement dust, noise, and crumbling pieces of the window frame.

The former sheriff quickly hoisted himself into the hole left by the breakage and fell into the cold, snowy night.

Cather spotted a drowsy deputy from the outlaw faction poking his head through the door to the jail. "Here's a horse, Sheriff. While our men are distracting the guard, you high-tail it out of here. Go somewhere, get someone to listen to you, and get us some help. We'll probably have to kill that guard so that we don't bring suspicion on ourselves. Otherwise, we're dead men. As it is, John Williams is going to be mad, so please don't be forever bringing back help. I hate to think what Williams will do."

Sheriff Swift, Cather, and another man rode quietly to the outskirts of town while the deputy was being handled. But it didn't take long for a sentry at the perimeter of the area the gang controlled to spot them.

"Where do you three think you're going at this time of night?" the outlaw asked.

Will Cather answered in a drunken drawl, while the sheriff, hiding his head, and the other man, circled the sentry. "We was jus' out for a little ride. We musta lost our way."

As the last word was spoken, the third man looped a wire over the outlaw's head and cut into his throat. He died without emitting a sound and fell from his horse, the sound of that covered by the hooves of the sheriff's horse as it left the scene.

Will and the other man turned back toward town, only concerned with being with their families for the night. They wondered about the consequences of their actions.

The next morning, Les dispatched a few of the young men to track the sheriff. They returned in less than a week, unable to locate his path in the continuing snow. The escape went unresolved. But John's revenge on Lander was a severe as could be expected.

"The old sheriff didn't make his escape by himself," John said. He stood on the boardwalk, glaring at the people in the town meeting. "He may not even have been the one who killed my men. There's no way I can find out who did this. I'm sure only the people involved know, and they aren't likely to tell me." John looked at Gary on his right and Lan on his left. "It doesn't matter to me who did it. Shooting any one of you is just as much a pleasure as any other." John drew his gun, zeroed in on a lady in the crowd, and gunned her down. "Don't pull another stunt like this."

Tears poured down the faces of the next of kin and friends of the murdered woman. But no one wailed. Everyone in town knew reaction would continue the slaughter. The people recoiled while the outlaw leaders walked away.

"Now we have to worry about what that sheriff is going to pull," John said to his fellow outlaws. "I told you we should have shot him."

Lan and Gary hung their heads and split from John's company.

Aside from occasional outbursts of resistance to their control, the outlaws had experienced few problems running the town. When situations arose that required reinforcement of their rules, the gang used lessons, such as the one following the sheriff's escape, to demonstrate the futility of fighting back and to remind the townsfolk of the ruthlessness of John Williams.

Little by little, the citizens came to accept occasional indignities, and the outlaws protected the town from disrupting forces from the outside. There were no Indian raids, no cattle wars, and no railroad crews overrunning the town. Lander experienced none of the things that were happening to the rest of the territory. The Williams Gang was the law in Lander and thereabout, and everybody in surrounding towns seemed to know it instinctively. The gang handled skirmishes fairly, and the citizens were thankful for that. Only interference with the gang brought unconditional retaliation.

It took time, almost another entire year, but the town eventually accepted the fact that compliance was their only choice. Their hopes that the sheriff of the old days would someday come riding to their rescue died as the months wore on. Obviously, he had saved his own neck and was not coming back. Some even thought the Williams Gang had found him and killed him.

"Sure, there are different people in charge," the people of Lander told each other. "Except for the 'taxes' the gang collects, things ain't a whole lot different."

Even the drunks in the saloons agreed.

The town's squabbles were replaced by bored tantrums from the gang. Appearances were much the same as before the Williams Gang took over, but the restlessness of the gang, caused by the peacefulness of their lives, was reflected in the tolerated outbursts by its members. Even as the controls on the town relaxed, flare-ups occurred.

"Let her down," a young husband said to one of the young gang members who had picked the woman up by the waist. "That's my wife. Leave her alone."

"You're lucky I'm not John Williams," the young outlaw said. "If I were, you'd be dead already." The outlaw ripped the woman's dress from her shoulders. Her husband's interference obviously had pushed him over the edge. He tossed the woman over his shoulder and carried her out the door.

The confused and terrified husband fought with the outlaw as he walked, but he knew he could lose his life, as well as his wife's, if he persisted. He followed the outlaw as he took her into the hotel and up to his room. Then the husband stopped at the doorway and held his face in his hands as his wife screamed.

The periodic breaks in the tranquility of life helped to build the anger of those who railed at the thought of the outlaws having control.

"You can see what I'm talking about. You all see it," a former town leader whispered to a small group of men in a saloon. "We don't have any say about how much of our money they take or how much of their nonsense we have to take. Things may be peaceful most of the time, but we've got no hope for it getting any better. They're outlaws. How can we tolerate this?"

After that, some of the men began to meet secretly.

"I can't believe what we're putting up with," one man said at a meeting. "And I can't believe the telegraph company actually bought their story about us voting to stay off the line, but they did."

"Let's face it," another one said. "We're stuck."

Indeed, the gang continued to act as outlaws. But if the townsfolk of Lander thought they were getting the worst of it, they would have been surprised at what the neighboring towns were experiencing.

The gang constantly worked to expand their holdings, always stressing to the conquered how lucky they were to now be under the *protection* of the Williams Gang. No one would dare bother the ranchers or townspeople with the gang in charge.

Truly, Lander did fair far better than the rest of central Wyoming. However, the forces of discontent still sought to erode the structure of the outlaw organization.

BADMAN, Polzin

Marcia regretted turning John in to the law. Shortly after the unsuccessful attack on the hideout, her fear that John would be killed was replaced by shame over betraying the man she loved.

In the two years after the battle, neither John nor Marcia tried to see the other. On Marcia's part, the avoidance was a matter of not being able to face him. How could she?

John wasn't sure what he would do if he ever saw Marcia again. He knew she was still at the ranch, and he couldn't deny he still had feelings for her. But he didn't want to gamble that the sight of her wouldn't bring on a rage he would later regret. (That sort of concern only fit John's psyche where Marcia was involved.) So he steered clear of Marcia, while continuing his frequent rampages. He used women for his pleasure, at his whim. All the while, he purposefully avoided any thoughts about Marcia.

During the two years following the siege on the outlaw hideout, things settled down in Lander. However, the distinction between townspeople and outlaws was never forgotten, by either faction, but both sides settled into a routine.

While ranchers came to town more freely as time passed, Marcia never did. She sent for her supplies instead. When her neighbors delivered them to her, she heard enough about the Williams Gang to reinforce her desire to remain outside their contact zone.

There were rumors about her involvement with John Williams circulating. Marcia knew that the neighbors and passing peddlers didn't know if the rumors were true but they suspected they were. Thus, Marcia made herself an unfamiliar sight to everyone. With additional time, she hoped she would become comfortable with the idea that she had done the right thing by helping the sheriff's posse, even though it was at her own heart's expense.

Marcia began hearing rumors that authorities on the outside were making plans to oust the outlaws.

"The old sheriff hasn't given up," one of her neighbors told her. "We don't want those hoodlums in town to know, but he's coming back. He's had a difficult time trying to stir up some interest with other authorities. He wants to make sure his return to Lander is a triumph. To him, time is not as important as making the necessary arrangements."

One day, Sheriff Swift showed up at Marcia's ranch house.

After sitting down, he said, "Marcia, I appreciate all the help you gave me with the raid on the gang's hideout. I want to be sure you know that. In case you've ever wondered, it wasn't me who spread the word that you were the woman who turned on John Williams. I tried to keep your involvement secret. But you know how that goes."

"I understand, Sheriff. Thank you."

Swift nodded. "I need your help again. You know more about John than anybody else. There might be some things you can tell me that will help us get him this time."

"Sheriff, I don't want to help you this time." Marcia rubbed her hands together and looked away from the Sheriff's face. "You'll have to get what you need somewhere else."

"That's the thing, ma'am. As much as everyone around here hates the Williams Gang, no one else wants to help us either. They're all afraid of what will happen if they help. What they don't understand is that if they help us catch him, nothing will happen to them. John Williams will no longer be a threat."

Marcia rocked in her rocking chair for a moment without saying anything. She stared out a window and then turned to face Swift. "Your track record of catching John isn't exactly stellar, is it? So of course townspeople are afraid of the consequences of helping you. They don't have a lot of faith in your ability to catch him, no matter how much information they provide. And they have seen too many friends or loved ones gunned down for lesser reasons. I'm sorry, Sheriff. I'm not going to help you."

The sheriff left Marcia's ranch house.

Over the next few months, revenge became Lander's legally installed sheriff's sole motivating factor in life.

"We can't worry about Lander and the Williams Gang right now," Major Johnson, the cavalry commander at Fort Bridger told him. "There's a gold rush on at South Pass, if you haven't heard. It's all this detachment can do to keep those miners and claim jumpers from killing each other."

"But Lander is in the clutches of the most notorious outlaw gang in the West," Swift said. "How can you just sit back and let it continue?"

"I don't hear a lot of complaints from the residents. Besides, you, of all people, should know how much time and effort it would take to capture that gang." The commander leaned back in his chair behind the desk. "The Cheyenne are upset about the gold rush. Red Cloud's treaty is being broken on both sides. We're two steps from general Indian war . . . I just can't take on anything else. What's more, it's too hot." He wiped his neck with his kerchief. "If you can get me transferred somewhere cool back East, then maybe I'll try to help you. Otherwise, take your problem somewhere else."

Sheriff Swift looked straight at the commander. "The governor has got Washington breathing down my neck to get rid of the outlaw element so that this territory can be respectable enough for people to settle here. Everybody's pushing for statehood . . ."

"I know," Johnson replied. "But my orders come from Washington. I'm not going to send my men into that suicide charge against the Williams Gang. I'll keep the governor happy. I'll round up his outlaws; although, it seems he thinks anybody who isn't a cattleman is an outlaw. But I'm not going after the Williams Gang. From what I hear, the area around Lander is relatively peaceful. Go see the governor. Maybe he'll help you round up some non-federal help."

A trip to Fort Steel brought Swift a similar response.

Meanwhile, the system of the corrupt in power, not only in Lander but also throughout the territory, stayed healthy. The ranchers controlled the range for their cattle, throttling the sheep herders and tearing down the fences of the "dirt farmers." Unlike the cattle ranchers, the Williams Gang was unchallenged. Each of the gang leaders controlled a small army of younger men — a regiment of his own.

Art Todd enjoyed being able to work on his safecracking trade and often traveled unnoticed outside the Williams Gang's area of control.

Ron Stone ran a rustling operation, pulling cattle from distant ranches or drives in progress. Rather than taking the herds to Lander, he drove them to the nearest Union Pacific railhead, adding money to the gang's coffers without injuring the community of Lander. This operation also added fuel to the range war, without any outsiders ever knowing that the Williams Gang was behind it or that one of its members was ranging far outside its safe haven.

Steve Perkins, the "sheriff," kept the local ranchers in line. He saw to it that an occasional ranch burned down when a rancher failed to cooperate with the gang. That gained cooperation from the rest of the ranchers for a while. On the surface, the burnings seemed to be just another event in the range war.

John and Lan were just happy not to be bothered with minor issues that surfaced naturally. The town "officials," headed by Gary, capably took care of them.

The members of the gang lived high and happily. But time was ticking, and the men were getting older. That posed a new set of problems.

"That ridiculous gold rush at South Pass has us right in the middle of traffic from Dakota to the new strike," John said to Lan as they were riding side by side with Gary on one of the touring trips they made to observe their kingdom. The horses seemed to enjoy the outings as much as the riders, straining to take their head whenever possible. "It's getting tough to control the town. We don't just need sentries anymore; we can't stop all the people who are coming. Everybody's got guns again, and all kinds of people have left town. Our little operation certainly isn't secret anymore, and it's falling apart."

As John's realization that he was losing control of the town grew, he couldn't help but wonder how much longer their authority would go uncontested. "The people here don't care who runs the town," he continued. "At least the Cheyenne and Shoshone raids are keeping the outside law too busy to give us any trouble. All these newcomers are a pain to deal with. We're supposed to be in charge here . . . I'm supposed to be in charge, and I can't do anything about . . ." John stopped as a thought crossed his mind. "Maybe we should just start shooting strangers on sight. The word would get out to avoid Lander."

"Not too much hope of that," Lan said. "With the big push to get people to settle in Wyoming so we can meet the population requirement to become a state, everyone's coming out here. A lot of shootings might just be what it would take to draw unwanted attention from the statehood crowd."

"Who wants to become a state? This place is getting too civilized and dull already. What is the world coming to? I don't like it. I want it the way it was. And that do-gooder sheriff never gives up either. I understand he's finally got some federal attention. I wish I could keep going like I used to. I could ride all night, slug my way through a couple of saloon brawls, and still draw faster than any man who dared face me. Back then, that old sheriff wouldn't have dared. But, I'm getting too old for that."

"We'll need more men in the gang," Lan said. "We're getting outnumbered. Some of the old boys—you know, the ones we added for the big battle at the hideout four years years ago —have deserted us and gone to the gold fields. We've had a few killed, and there's too many undesirables around. They're not fit to be in the gang, and we can't keep them in line without more good men on our side. We tried to assimilate the disruptive element, but that was a disaster. That leaves no solution but to control them with more manpower."

John looked at Gary and saw a wry look on his face.

"Who wants to join the gang?" Gary said. "Everybody does what they want now. There's no prestige in being a member of the Williams Gang. Those troublemakers were the only ones interested, and all they wanted was a place to belong."

"We don't need any more boys," John said. "Nobody's fighting us anymore."

"You've forgotten what Sheriff Swift is up to," Lan said.

Governor Campbell, no longer willing to look the other way, sensed the best chance there ever had been to end the outlaws' hold on Lander. In the face of the mounting statehood movement, the governor was ready to thwart the outlaw element throughout the territory. He repeatedly made his requests to the cavalry installations at Fort Laramie and Fort Washakie and the representatives from Washington, DC. His requests were finally approved.

If statehood was coming, Campbell wanted to look good when it happened. One of the best things he could do for his image was clean up the outlaw element. Washington couldn't argue with his intentions, and the wheels were set in motion.

The governor and his representatives from Washington, DC, old cronies responsible for getting him appointed territorial governor, worked out plans. They were joined by Sheriff Swift and his group of dissidents from Lander, including Will Cather, who had eventually been able to leave town. Sheep herders and others, many of whom weren't cattle ranchers and who normally opposed Governor Campbell, also drummed up support in the name of the statehood cause. The federal cooperation did no harm to the confidence needed for citizens to volunteer to be a part of the program to confront the gang.

"We can't just attack the gang," the old sheriff told those concerned at a meeting in the capitol building. "The outlaws will get word of what we're up to, and they'll high-tail it up to their hideout in the rimrocks. And even if we did manage to surprise them in Lander, lots of innocent people would get hurt. How would we tell who was in the gang and who wasn't?" The sheriff lowered his eyes. The shame of losing so many men during his previous attempt to stop the gang threatened to overwhelm him. "We've already tried to overrun them once in their hideout, and that didn't work . . ." He kicked at the tiled floor.

"So what makes you think we can be successful this time?" someone asked.

"The gang isn't as well organized as it was then. It's bigger and spread out all over. But we can't risk failure. This needs to be planned thoroughly. We've got to assure success this time."

Swift knew it was impossible to surprise the gang with a sneak attack. Overpowering the gang in their hideout wouldn't work either. But he also knew there were Williams Gang sympathizers, or even gang members, in the local cavalry detachments. So, why not plant some enemies in the gang's ranks?

He knew it wouldn't be easy. The gang had built up a sizeable amount of respect by their accomplishments. Life in Lander had been relatively peaceful. The Williams Gang had developed an aura of romanticized fantasy.

"The thing we must do—the only way to stop this outlaw band—is to quietly put federal agents afield to infiltrate the hideout. The time we spend infiltrating will have no value in itself, since only the eight leaders of the gang are in a position to hurt the operation. But if we infiltrate the hideout, we can attack them from inside once they retreat for safety."

～✦ ✦～

The gang noticed no suspicious buildup of men at Army installations or law enforcement agencies. Men who joined the gang and then disappeared weren't missed. They were assumed to have left for South Pass. The additions to the outlaw army hadn't been going well overall anyway. Even some of the old-timers were leaving stealthily. These included Ron Stone, who had long been disgruntled over being ignored or overlooked. He set out on his own to form another gang—one in the northern part of Dakota Territory, far from John Williams.

The small number of sentries who were watching the hideout to keep it free of intruders saw only those who were ostensibly their pals. They just ushered the visitors in and out of the archway. No notice was paid to their actions or their disappearances. Everything seemed normal, and the hideout was generally empty. Only occasional visits from the leaders interrupted the serenity of the landscape. However, this was not often since the leaders of the gang preferred the comforts of town to the austere living conditions of the basin.

The occasional stranger who passed through Lander drew no more attention than the gold rush crowd. Appearances were normal in town, and the gang went about business as usual.

The infiltrating lawmen joining as gang members found themselves assigned to the least desirable duty—that of guarding the lonely hideout. Only an occasional lizard or a snake or two darted among the rocks to ease their boredom. But little by little, the agents disappeared into the landscape. They dug holes in the ground. They built rock walls that blended into the natural lay of the land. They used every creative idea at their disposal to find hiding places, always working at night and in silence and independence. They founded their refuges over an expanded stretch of time so that their efforts would go unnoticed.

The agents came prepared. Since they did not want to alert the gang, they arrived at different intervals. This allayed suspicions that the curious fellow sentries might have had if a group of new members had joined up all at once. The agents just had to wait for opportunities to enter the forbidden hideout without being observed.

Eventually, over fifty men successfully went into hiding within the confines of the hideout. It took over a month, but with previously coordinated movement, this collection of federal lawmen independently took position. It was the largest gathering of marshals ever assembled.

The gang was totally unaware of the lawmen's activities. The gang was blissfully secure in its belief of invincibility and constantly more and more disorganized and careless. Without their knowing it, the safe harbor had turned into a potential death trap for the outlaws.

Sustained on army rations and well supplied with ammunition from the gang's own stash, the government forces waited for the right moment. The gang had to be made to retreat to the basin hideout.

The cavalry regiment at Fort Laramie began a massive buildup. The buildup was immediately noticed and reported to the Williams Gang. Concern spread among the leaders. The leaked information indicated that the Williams Gang was indeed the objective. Gary, John, and Lan called the other leaders together in the mayor's office.

"Well, I guess the sheriff finally got some federal attention alright," Steve said.

"I wish I could laugh this activity off," Gary said. "I'd like to say, 'We'll show them just like the last time.' But this isn't a sheriff's posse made up of ranchers and shopkeepers. These are trained soldiers. The men commanding this operation won't be as easy to outguess as the old sheriff. We have an old and deteriorated Gatling gun, some rifles, and a few other weapons. The cavalry has everything we've got and much more. They're probably better at using them too. Worst of all, they may have some new weaponry that would drastically shift the advantage to their side."

"But we've got your military mind and the hideout," John said. He had come to trust Gary—maybe too much.

"Their colonel finished West Point," Gary said. "I dropped out . . . washed out . . . after two years."

Around the room, there was silence. John's long unanswered question about Gary's background finally had been cleared up.

"But you're right, we do have the hideout. There will surely be a long siege. They won't fall for simple tricks like we used on the posse last time. The hideout is not necessarily safe from the cavalry."

John looked around and saw concern on the other men's faces.

"They can lob cannon fire in on us. They can demolish the rimrocks and bury us in the rubble. We need to have an escape plan ready, just in case."

"I'll get the boys busy carting provisions and ammo out to the basin," Lan said. "I'll see if we can round up some new weapons. Carbines would be nice for rapid fire. Maybe we can get some other new stuff too."

John looked up in interest.

"Do you think a new style cannon would be useful against a large group like a cavalry regiment?" Lan asked. He grinned.

"Where could we get a cannon of any kind?" John replied.

"Where else? From the Army."

"Don't go getting our boys cut down trying to steal a cannon," Gary said. "We need all the manpower we can get, and we need it right here. We'll be outnumbered as it is."

"I have a plan," Lan said. "Don't worry. We won't lose any men getting the cannon."

Al spoke up for the first time. "There is another option. We could all split up and go our separate ways. We don't need to fight it out."

The comment drew nothing but looks of disbelief. Running would bring the wrath of John — they might as well die trying to save his dream.

Lan turned away from the others and headed out the door to the street. He could no longer envision life without the Williams Gang. Maybe the gang needed a little shake-up like this. Then things would get back to the way they used to be. The gold rush was dying. It hadn't lasted long. The South Pass strike hadn't been that big. Soon there wouldn't be so many strangers coming through Lander, and the gang would be back in complete control. A new century was coming and the Williams Gang would be ready for it. He grabbed the reins to his horse and mounted, on his way to steal a cannon.

BADMAN, Polzin

The leaders set out on their missions to prepare. Lan went to get his cannon. Gary and John went to work on plans to acquire some other army weapons. There were rumors that some of the Cheyenne had a captured cache that might be available. Gary and John also began devising a plan of defense for the hideout and an escape plan in case all else failed.

Les and Art were assigned the duty of stockpiling food and supplies. They went from building to building in Lander, confiscating anything they needed. It was the type of activity they hadn't needed for a long time, and the citizenry didn't take kindly to it.

"We haven't caused you any trouble," Jim Curry, the general store owner said. "You can't just come in here and take what you want. I pay your taxes. Me and the rest of the town treat you guys like kings. Where's the call to start taking away our means of livelihood?"

"We've always had that call," Art said. "You had better shut up old man, or John Williams will hear about your lip."

The shopkeeper swallowed his words. John's ruthlessness was still enough to quell resistance. No one wanted a visit from the man himself.

At the bank, Les was confronted by obstruction as well.

"What do you need money for?" the bank president, George Fredricks, said. "You take everything you want, and we pay you to leave us alone."

"We need to buy things that aren't available here in Lander," Les began to explain in his usual slow fashion. "We don't want to take a chance on losing any men by taking them elsewhere . . ."

Art arrived to settle the dispute quickly and efficiently. "Les, you don't need to explain anything." Then, turning to the banker, he made sure it was understood that there would be no more questions. "I want $10,000 in currency. Now! I don't want any backtalk or delays."

"But that's a lot of money," Fredricks said.

"Mister, how would you like to be dinner for a coyote?"

Art's question needed no answer, and there was none. The banker rounded up the money and handed it over. "That's just about everything we've got."

Art swaggered from the bank with a heavy feeling. He still balked at violence and danger. He certainly didn't like the possibilities of the coming confrontation with the cavalry, but he had no choice but to stand with the gang. He enjoyed the feeling of power he experienced as one of the leaders of the Williams Gang. He needed only to threaten violence to have his way. On a day-to-day basis, he was living a lot higher on the hog, and he liked it that way. These were the best times of his life.

"Come on, Les. Let's see what else we can round up," Art said.

Les followed him like a sheepdog. Art thought he was not so different than him. Art knew Les stayed with the gang because of John's threats to track down and kill him if he left. The lowly sentries and other gang members didn't matter much to John. But if the leaders fell out, John would not react well.

Sure, Ron Stone had left and gone far away. But Art wasn't sure he was safe. Someday, John might find him. And the defection gave John fuel for an "I told you so" harangue with Lan. After all, it had been Lan who vouched for Ron in the first place. Art had no intention of attempting Ron's feat, nor of pushing John's appreciation of him like Lan did.

Looking at Les, he believed he had to say something to him. "One of these days, Les, you're going to learn how to handle things like that." But, Art was fully aware Les could never change, but he also knew Les' ego needed a boost.

Les had little trouble getting the weapons, ammunition, and such after that. Newcomers to town were hit hardest. That showed the benefit of cooperating with the gang over the years, like long-time residents had. Still, every home and business in Lander had a visit.

Les knew his mind was not as strong as Gary's, the gang member he most looked up to. But he knew he had value. He just went about doing what he was sent to do and allowed nothing to deter him from the path to obtaining that objective.

He would have settled the problem with the banker in his own way if Art had not shown up. There would have been violence, and Les would not have been the victim. He had developed a reputation of his own for ruthlessness. In reality, the usually jolly cook had no room in his mentality for making value judgments. He set out to do something and didn't think twice about what he had to do to get it done. If he was obstructed, his temper was a match for John's.

People in town knew only too well that where Ron Stone could have been put off with a bluff, Les Brass would strike down resistance with a beefy arm—regardless of the sex or age of the resister, as one woman found out.

"I want the tablecloths and towels," Les said to the waitress in the café. "Throw in any guns you've got here too."

"All the tablecloths and towels? But what will we use then?"

Les rubbed his bushy eyebrows.

"I'll have to talk to the owner. I'm just the waitress."

Les backhanded her across the face, sending her flying across the room. She landed in a heap against the counter.

The owner came running, and Les screamed his orders again. The owner wisely rounded up the linens and guns before attending to the girl on the floor.

"We need these for bandages and stuff," Les said. He left the café with a grin on his stubbled face. He'd done his job.

Al and Steve made the rounds of the livery stable and nearby ranches to gather horses and tack. If an escape became necessary, transportation had to be available. The horses were corralled at various points in the area outside of the hideout. Each corral was stocked heavily enough that any one of them could accommodate the entire leadership of the gang. No provision was made for the rank and file gang members.

Some of Les' young army appropriated livestock as well, to ensure a continuing source of food if a siege outlasted their supplies. Other young men under the rein of Les obtained a few buggies and wagons, which they used to haul things and then kept for any future uses.

The dry weather of late spring worked to the advantage of the outlaws. The ground was solid, the wagons easy to pull, and the spring calves plentiful.

"What do you mean, you're taking my entire spring calving?" an unfortunate rancher said.

"I mean, we're taking all your newborns and herding them out of here," Al said.

"But they can't be driven. They're too young."

"Oh, we won't be taking them far," Al said. "We'll just be taking every one of them. Don't give me any trouble." Al drew his gun and signaled his men to start cutting out the calves. He hated force almost as much as John loved it. But he often managed to get by without any actual violence. Usually, when there was violence in his operations, it was self-defense. "You'll have another calving next year," he added.

The man could only stand and watch his herd being divided. He and his ranch hands were disarmed and helpless.

Al and Steve always approached their contacts in a manner consistent with their personalities. Al politely explained the gang's need and promised better fortunes for the future. Then, patiently, both he and Steve would remind those who initially refused that they had no choice.

Steve stood his ground and backed up Al against adversity. But on his own, he never backed down from resistance. He reduced two ranches in the area to ashes. The gang's objectives were met, and then the destruction followed as a lesson to others that the Williams Gang would not allow interference.

When the gang reassembled at the hideout, initial conversations were casual, with no mention of the dangerous, imminent future. Every member of the gang knew the cavalry was ready to move. Now was the time to retreat. The basin would be their home for a while.

"Boy, Les is sure the loyal dog." John laughed. "Just like you said, Lan. Art says he follows him around like a sheep."

Everybody laughed. Les had long been serving as sergeant of the guard over the sentries and other infantrymen of the gang's army. It was a job the top leaders felt he could handle and that would make him feel good about his position in the gang. He had done his job well. His sheepishness didn't prevent him from leading the inexperienced and anxious-to-please boys who cherished being a part of the notorious Williams Gang and the spoils it provided. The "privates" of the gang also knew Les was backed up by the vicious John Williams, whom they looked up to with awe but feared.

"You guys know he just appreciates what we've got here," Art said. "He's never lived so good. Neither have I. I feel like I'm part of something."

"You are," Gary said.

"Well, we can thank Les for some of that good living," Art said. "He's put a lot of good meals in our bellies."

Light laughter broke out among the gang leaders.

"Well, we've got our infantry all comfy on the rimrocks," John said to the group. "The positions are stocked. Everything is set up just the way we want it. All we have to do now is wait for the cavalry charge."

"We still haven't finished working out our escape plan," Gary said. "We need to see about a lot of details before the attack comes."

"Yeah, well, we can't do anything right now, in the dark," John said. "And I'm sleepy, so I'm off to bed." Gary, Lan, and others had been handling most of the planning for some time, and John was fine with that. Who needed the stress—especially considering how well their plans were turning out?

The six men finished their cups of coffee, dealt with their bedtime business, and crawled into their bedrolls.

The seventh leader, Les, had bedded down among his soldiers in the rimrocks at the top of the basin. Art was scheduled to awaken him when the next shift of sentries was due to take over.

The outlaws unknowingly nested with vipers. The federal agents within the hideout remained hidden, silently waiting.

Weeks went by for the agents without any word to move on the outlaws. The agents subsisted on jerky and water. Occasionally, a minute raid on the gang's stores went unnoticed.

John and Gary prevailed upon Lan to relate his operation for obtaining the cannon and new weapons from Fort Laramie. It was kept a secret from all but those directly involved. Even John and Gary did not know how Lan planned to acquire the items, but they had his promise not to lose any manpower in the operation. He also assured the others that his activity would not draw attention to the gang's preparations to confront the cavalry. That was why Lan had selected Fort Laramie instead of one of the closer military installations. So, pulling the secrets of the operation eventually became campfire discussion.

Lan and Art handpicked their men and then entered the fort late at night, drawing the attention of only two guards.

"Open up," Lan said to the guard above the gate. "We've got sick children here in the wagon."

"Open up," the guard said to his partner below.

Since the fort had the only doctor in the area, it was not uncommon for civilians to seek medical help at the fort. Only the hour was unusual. But sickness happens at all times of the day or night, so no suspicions were aroused. Besides, the visitors were white, not Indians. Lan expected these facts would lull the soldiers into a relaxed frame of mind. He was correct, to the soldiers' regret.

The two cavalry guards escorted the wagon into the compound, and Lan distracted the guards with conversation about taking unseen children to the post doctor, drawing the guards' attention in the direction of the buildings. Then the guards were struck with gun butts from behind by other outlaws.

"Art, the armory is over there—by the flag pole and ceremonial cannon." Lan pointed.

"Yeah, I figured it was the building with the bars and locks," Art said. "I guessed you picked me to come along on this errand because you might need some locks opened." Art had joined Lan's group en route, after he had completed his work in Lander with Les, delivering their booty.

"Load up the wagon with ammunition for the cannon and everything else in the armory you think we can use," Lan said. "I'll hook up the cannon to the team of horses."

Before long, the wagon was loaded without awakening any other soldiers. They tied extra horses behind the wagon on which the ceremonial cannon was mounted. Only then did the noise of the rolling wagons draw any attention.

Still, only one sleepy-eyed pony soldier wandered past the outlaws on his way to the latrine. He rubbed his eyes.

"Evening," Lan said.

The soldier nodded without comprehension and continued on his way, not really caring about anything but reaching his destination and relieving his bladder.

The outlaws pushed the gates open from the inside, and the wagons pulled away. Once they were beyond the gates, they increased their pace. The next change of guards wouldn't come until dawn, and the raiding party would be halfway back to the hideout before reveille would awaken the fort to its losses. Lan smiled. The commandant would only be able to wonder at who had taken his cannon and other arms.

Lan and his team made it safely back to the hideout with no known pursuit. And with so many tracks crisscrossing the terrain, it would be impossible for anyone to determine which tracks led to the cannon's destination.

The outlaws soon successfully installed the cannon in the appointed spot. The other new weapons, principally carbines, were passed out among the men. The hideout was once again ready for an onslaught.

Gary did not make the mistake of underestimating the caliber of effort the cavalry would use against them. Still, he believed their chances were not bad. If they could close the battle before it became a long siege, there was a chance the Army would lose interest in an extended deployment. They still had Indians and other problems requiring their manpower.

However, Gary's assessment did not take into account the hidden men inside the rock bowl. He had no way of knowing that the government forces had no intention of taking the fortress from the outside at the cost of many lives. Their entire operation was geared toward driving the gang into the rocks and then attacking from within.

The first step of Gary's plan was successful. The gang was ensconced in the rock hideout. Then a few more days went by while they made last-minute preparations. Word got to the gang members that the people in Lander were talking. They knew why they suddenly had been freed from gang members and hoped for an army victory.

Then, one autumn day, a report came in that the regiment from Fort Laramie, the same one Lan had stolen the cannon from, was on the move toward Lander. They had gotten the word that the Williams Gang had made a complete retreat to their readied stronghold in the rocks, and the army suspected the gang was responsible for stealing their weapons.

At the hideout, everything was ready for the confrontation. The agents remained hidden; although, the livestock in the area had forced them to dig deeper into their shelters. They had to avoid detection by causing unexplained rousing of the young cattle.

The gang stashed its horses at hidden corrals before the final retreat to the hideout. The supplies and armament were in place and sufficient to last for a fairly lengthy siege. The capabilities from livestock and agricultural work under Les' leadership gave them the means of resisting even longer.

Inside the bowl, Gary and the other leaders finalized the escape plan designed to avert disaster in a worst-case scenario.

Gary said, "I think our best chance for an escape, if the hideout were overrun would be a ladder-like affair situated on a rock wall on the far side of the basin, away from the entrance. We can carve steps between levels of the spiral trail and then construct a wooden frame ladder to reach the top of the wall from the upper level of the trail. That will give us a quick way to get free from the bottom of the basin and to the top of the rim."

"But if we're surrounded and being overrun, we'd be sitting on top of the rocks, waiting to get picked off," Lan said.

"Just hold on a minute, Lan," Gary said. "At the top of the rim, on the inside, we will assemble a rope ladder to lower down the outside of the rimrocks in an emergency. We can't make it permanent because we would be giving the lawmen a way to get in here." Gary rolled out a piece of paper he had been carrying under his arm. "But once we drop down over the rim, we could move toward the northwest side of the bowl. There's a large rock formation here." He pointed to a spot on his handmade map. "All around the rock, there is fairly soft dirt. We're going to dig a short tunnel, under the rock a little ways, so that we can come up beyond the lines of the assaulting forces. I've checked it out. We can do it. We've got some lumber here, and we can rip up shacks and wagons for more, if we need to, so that we can make the tunnel safe. I've already got Les bringing us some digging tools. We'll do the digging ourselves. Our men won't know about this."

Something clicked in John's head. "Wait a minute," he said. "Who says we're going to do all this? What makes you think it's alright for you to turn us into laborers?" The building excitement was getting to John. Similar details had been handled by others for months and never drawn his notice. Usually he realized most decisions were better left to Gary or Lan. But John still bridled from time to time when they left him out of the decisions. And the truth was, while others were feeling fear, John was just getting wound up.

"John, have you got some better ideas?" Gary asked, making sure he spoke as softly as possible.

John stared at the West Point dropout, obviously seething. Then he turned away. "No, you know I don't."

"We're not taking over," Lan said. "We're just doing what's best for all of us. You're the boss, we all know that. That's the way we want it." Lan looked at Gary.

Gary nodded in confirmation. "It's your dream we're trying to save, John," he said. "We could ride out of here right now without endangering our lives. If we killed you, we wouldn't have to worry about you tracking us for some future vendetta. But we're all working to hold this kingdom of yours—together."

"Go ahead with what you're doing," John said. He walked away.

Gary worked out the details. Les was dispatched for meals. The shovels he brought were put to use at night, and the progress was slow. Still, the work on the steps, ladder, and tunnel continued. The leaders did the work themselves because they didn't want even their own men to know about their plans. The less the others knew, the better.

You could never tell where a weak link in an organization would occur. Someone in the gang could be waiting for a chance to become a big man and turn against them. Thus, many of the newest members had limited knowledge, at best. The highest leaders drew comfort in knowing the lower level gang members couldn't hurt them. John had always run the gang that way. It was hard to dispute his wisdom, if that's what it was.

To the best of anyone's knowledge, the privates in the Williams Gang had never set foot inside the rimrocks, even to deliver goods brought from town. Les, Art, or Ron had always met them at the archway to take the items down the spiral trail to the main camp. Some may have wandered in during the years of disuse but certainly not many.

The activities of the leaders confused the ensconced agents, who were forced to stay concealed. They had no idea what the activity in the basin was for and couldn't chance investigating. Thus, they were aware of some of the work on the escape route but not aware of its purpose. And they had no knowledge of the tunnel work going on outside the rimrocks because their positions did not allow them to see over the wall around them.

The government men in seclusion found it difficult to remain unseen and leave no sign of their presence. But they managed. They buried the residue from their food, as well as their alimentary discharges. They were lean, underfed, anxious, bored, and out of touch but ready to go into active mode when the time was right.

After two days on the march, the cavalry's leading formation split into three company-sized units and turned toward the foothills, without ever entering Lander. They towed their heavy weaponry behind the columns with teams of horses.

The cavalry knew the route to the rimrock haven of the outlaws. They had supplies and a supply line back to the fort, as well as the ability to draw needs from Lander and the closer forts. The unit was well equipped with weapons and full strength in manpower.

The full regiment was 15,000 men. Since they were strung out all the way back to Ft. Laramie, however, in various stages of combat readiness, only 8,000 men were in position to storm or besiege the outlaws. The support units, field hospital members, and quartermaster, would never approach the hideout—nor would the field officers or general officer who arrived from Washington. No one above company grade would be subjected to danger. The federal agents didn't know it, but they had much the same arrangement the outlaw gang had.

Finally, one morning, the sentries sent word down from the rimrocks that the enemy was in sight. The cavalry was approaching.

Les, Art, Steve, and Al were stationed around the rim to guide the activities of their army. They were the company-grade officers of the outlaws.

As the first riders entered the range of the newly acquired cannon, Les gave the signal to fire. The first shot fell short and sent the cavalrymen asunder. The scattered attackers reduced the effectiveness of the big gun. It would have been quite different if the first shot had hit the formed unit. But now the factor of surprise was over, and the army knew for sure that the outlaws had a cannon.

The soldiers did not fire back immediately, but the outlaws fired heavily with their long-range rifles. It seemed the outlaws had more ammunition on hand than the cavalry did. Les wondered if the army had been forced to stash supplies along the route of the march, all the way back to Ft. Laramie.

When they were strategizing, it seemed to Gary that the most applicable strategy under the circumstances was to use their heavy stocks and send a full barrage of fire into the attackers, so that is what they did.

As the army grew nearer, the outlaws added the creaky, old Gatling gun to the mix, sending riders toppling off their mounts. Some of the soldiers dove for cover, hiding behind rocks; others just hit the ground where they were. The government forces probably had planned on not losing many men, but it was obvious they had underestimated the firepower of the outlaws.

When the troops finally reached the skirt of the hill, they cautiously began creeping their way upward on all sides. Then they started returning fire from their fanned out positions as they reached the range of their carbines. As distance grew shorter, the outlaws began using their new rapid-fire carbines as well.

Inside the basin, the sounds of gunfire were no hint as to the progress of the battle.

"I've got to go up and see for myself," John said.

"That's not a good idea," Gary countered. "Steve just brought us a detailed report on the battle."

"That's not enough for me. I want in on the excitement."

"This isn't a game. We have to be careful, or our lives could end right here."

John stood up abruptly. He grabbed a rifle that was leaning against the sidewall of the lean-to and started up the trail.

Lan and Gary jumped to their feet.

"We'll go with you," Lan said. "It's better if we're together, so we'll all have the same information, in case we need to make some decisions."

A few minutes later, shadows started obscuring the figures hiding behind the rocks up and down the slope of the hill. An officer instructed the troops to start edging their way up the hill, under the cover of darkness. There was no maneuvering of the Gatling this time, for the lower levels were held in check by the cavalry's cannons and heavy weapons.

⁓❦⁓

John, Al, Gary, and Lan met near the top of the trail and took a position on the ground. They were exposed as they watched the landscape below them.

"Did you hear that?" Al asked. "I think I heard something moving inside the basin. I guess it was just an animal."

⁓❦⁓

Behind them, the government agents moved toward the main camp at the bottom of the basin. The approach of nightfall, after the onset of battle, was their signal to move. From their well hidden positions, they converged in the darkness, on the spot they believed still contained the leaders of the gang.

Due to the noise of the battle, the agents were unaware that their quarry had slipped outside the confines of their trap. It had always been assumed that the leaders would congregate deep within the safety of the lean-to camp when danger was near. The agents had no reason to think that the men they sought would leave their hideout campsite. It was only John's desire to be where the action was that saved him and his close associates from quick extinction.

⁓❦⁓

Al's keen ears became aware of the more and more overt movement below them, even though the gunfire still rang sporadically through the night. "John, there's someone down there," Al whispered.

All four outlaws turned to stare into the gloom just as the agents made their gun-blazing plunge into the outlaws' main camp.

John, Al, Gary, and Lan lost no time scrambling for the prepared escape ladder.

"Signal Steve, Art, and Les that it's time to get out of here." Gary relayed to Al.

Al gave the predetermined signal for an emergency, and the other leaders hustled toward the escape ladder without question. Their departure did not draw attention or cause panic in the men manning the defenses. They were used to the leaders coming and going. Besides, they were quite occupied with fighting for their lives.

By the time the first of the leaders started up the ladder, the rest were close at their heels. The pinning fire of the cavalry, returned heavily by the outlaws, mingled in the closing darkness. And firing was still wildly riddling the makeshift buildings of the main camp at the bottom of the basin. It seemed whoever was down there was firing in random, rapid fire. They obviously wanted to leave no chance for the presumably trapped outlaws to escape or return fire. Al was grateful to be far above them, climbing the escape ladder to the top of the rimrocks.

"How did they get in here?" John asked.

"There must be about fifty of them." Al whistled in awe and fear.

"Shut up and keep moving," Gary said.

John's revolver flew from his holster, and Gary cowered on a lower rung of the ladder. The entire group stopped moving, gathering breaths in heaves.

John glared at Gary and then finally roared in insane laughter. "You traitors." He leveled his gun in the direction of the distant lawmen and fired. His shot didn't draw any attention. It was drowned by the surrounding din.

Lan quickly knocked John onto the flat, rock ledge at the top of the ladder. Lan tore the gun from John's hand and aimed it at him. "John, we can settle this later, but you're not going to get us all killed by drawing attention to us. Al and Gary, get into the tunnel." He looked at the two men, who were still frozen on the ladder.

John struggled to get up, knowing Lan wouldn't shoot him.

Lan continued to point the gun at John. "Save yourself. Use your head. Get into that tunnel. We've lost this battle, but we can get out alive. We'll have a chance to do all this again . . . if we get out of here now." Lan lowered the gun and let John get up to his feet.

John stood silently, staring at Lan. Then he turned and walked to the entrance of the tunnel, just as the last of the others disappeared into it.

⤞◎ ◎⤝

Al, Les, Art, Steve, and Gary came out the downhill end of the tunnel and turned to wait for the others. No one spoke. In total darkness, it was difficult to tell friend from foe. Silence seemed like a good idea.

When John, then Lan, emerged from the tunnel, they saw John promptly get down on the ground by Lan. They joined them. Lan was running the show and made no bones about it. He still held John's gun in his hand. Apparently, would have none of John's showboat tactics.

⤞◎ ◎⤝

"We've got to split up and get out of here on our own," Lan whispered above the gunfire.

John dusted his pants off and looked through the darkness toward Lan's voice. "How dare you—" John said.

"Shut up. We don't know where the soldiers are; they could be above or around us. And there's bound to be logistical support spread out all over. By the sounds of the gunfire, there are soldiers everywhere. We still have something working for us. They're under as much pressure as we are. These soldiers are scared too. They didn't expect us to escape. If they hear us, there's a good chance they'll think we're soldiers like them. That's what they'll want to think."

Lan turned toward John. "Get yourselves out of here, and we'll meet again. Make it to Carson City, Nevada. We're unknown there. Then you can settle your score with me, John. Maybe by then you'll be able to accept the fact that I saved your life. But then again, you might not make it to Nevada. You'll be on your own after we split up. There won't be anyone to look after you. Now, get going." He waved his hand to scatter the men.

The seven leaders of the Williams Gang spread out and crawled down the hill. Within a few feet, they lost track of each other. Around them, there was gunfire, followed by cannon fire that bombarded the rimrocks.

⤞◎ ◎⤝

The battle raged on for, ultimately, no purpose. The federal agents inside the hideout, not knowing that their prime quarry had escaped, occupied the main camp and held their ground to wait for morning. They had moved up and out from the bottom of the basin, as planned, but they were puzzled by the lack of bodies. They chose to sit tight until daylight could assist them in assessing the situation. Their moving around at night would make them targets for the outlaws—and maybe the cavalry too.

On the outside of the rim, the soldiers, whose plans had been altered by their success, were slowly overpowering the defenses. Before long, some of the men serving the Williams Gang crawled away in the darkness, in an attempt to survive. Some of the outlaws surrendered, but most lay dead in the barrage of the U.S. government's firepower.

The morning found many dead. Bodies from both sides lay around the stony fortress. Inside the basin, no sign was found of any of the leaders of the Williams Gang. The agents found the ladder and tunnel, but they did not find the men who built them.

BADMAN, Polzin

John Williams was surprised to find himself safely on the outskirts of Lander, Wyoming. He had to admit Gary's escape plan had probably saved his life. *The plan and Lan.*

One more stolen horse added to his outlaw record allowed him the chance to circle to the west and assault the Rockies. Instead of heading blindly for the prearranged meeting place, Carson City, he wandered aimlessly around the snow-covered Rockies. He was well aware the decision to meet in Carson City had not been his. He had no interest in rejoining his partners—for the time being. His thoughts turned toward Marcia, just as they did every time he got into a near-fatal situation. Torn between his desire to see her again and determination to forget her, John started a journey that lasted two full years.

He headed along the divide but stayed below the timberline. He spent many snowy nights curled up by a fire, with only a horse for company. From time to time, he would come to a town. Then he would pick up a few dollars in one way or another and take a break from the wilderness. Day to day, week to week, he wandered without drawing much attention.

He survived on what he could steal or what nature provided. It never occurred to him to get work and stay in one place, at least through the cold months. But he wondered what type of work he might be able to do when the weather got warmer, knowing that, realistically, there was no job he would do.

⚬⚬⚬

In Pueblo, Colorado, John found a pretty young girl who caught his fancy. "Hey, Missy," John said. "Do ya suppose ya could spare a hungry man a favor . . . and some food?"

"That depends what the favor is. The food I'm sure I can handle," she replied.

"I meant the food as the favor." John struggled to make sure he sounded kind. He didn't want to scare her off. "But if you want to throw in something else, I wouldn't say 'no.'"

The girl laughed gently. "We might see about that later. How about some food for now?"

John laughed, but not in his usual way. This laugh was lighter, less intimidating. They were in the café alone. The girl, who couldn't be more than fifteen, seemed to be running the place by herself. But the eyes she scanned John with were not fifteen-year-old eyes. It was obvious that the rugged, dirty maleness of John appealed to her.

"I'll get you some eggs and pancakes," she said.

"You know I can't pay," John said.

"I know. Just sit down." She disappeared into the kitchen.

A few minutes later, after John had removed his heavy coat and made himself comfortable, the girl brought out the food. John dug right in.

"My name's Denise," the girl said. She sat down across the table from him and watched him eat.

John looked up into her eyes and paused his gorging. "What are you looking at?"

"You," she said and laughed. "When you get a moment between

bites, tell me about yourself. How is it that you come to be so hungry and broke?"

"What's it to you?"

"Well, I did give you a free meal. You at least owe me some conversation."

"Alright," John said. He took another bite. "How about some coffee?"

Denise shuffled to her feet and went to get it.

When she returned, John said, "I'm a down-on-my-luck outlaw on the run for my life. There, you happy now?"

Denise poured his coffee into the cup he had turned right-side-up on the table. There was no fear or terror in her expression, but she obviously believed him. "So, outlaw, what are your plans after breakfast?"

"I haven't got any."

"Do you need a place to stay?"

John stopped eating and looked at Denise again. She was young, but she had the body and manner of a woman. "Yeah, I do."

Later, Denise took him to her living area, which was reached by an outside staircase behind the café. That day, they began an unlikely relationship, which lasted a length of time that neither of them would have thought possible when they first met. Denise was drawn to the much older, rugged man, and he was touched by her beauty and youth. But John showed her respect, as he had no woman other than Marcia.

Perhaps John was salving his wounded ego and pointless pride. His lifelong dream was gone. He had no gang, no hideout, no money—and he didn't have Marcia, the only woman he had ever loved. He had nothing. He was a failure.

Characteristically, John's restlessness could only be contained for so long. One night, he quietly stole away.

BADMAN, Polzin

John wandered aimlessly among the trees and rocks of the mountains. He had no immediate destination in mind. He just couldn't force himself to stay in one place. How he had done that while running things in Lander, he couldn't fathom. All he knew was that he was restless.

He didn't want to get to Carson City, and he didn't want to be alone. But his choices were to stay with Denise or to meet up with his gang in Nevada. Both choices left him unfulfilled.

John had no money. What little he had carried ran out days after he escaped the trap at the hideout. Aside from when he was staying with Denise, he lived off what he could shoot and cook in the open. But his bullets were disappearing too. That meant he had to make some kind of change in his activities—and soon. However, his mind just couldn't focus.

Sleeping under the stars one night, John began to think seriously of returning to Marcia. But he couldn't shake the fact that she had turned him in. Going back would only result in getting caught. Marcia was bent on reforming him—if she would have him at all now. The past held no future for him, and he knew it. Still, even though her betrayal inflamed his rage, his desire for her was hard to extinguish. That had even been true during his recent affair with Denise.

After a couple more days, John was tired of sleeping on the ground and of being cold, hungry, and short of cash. He started into a small town along the Wyoming border. He wandered up to the hotel, tied his horse to the rail out front, and stomped through the front doors. Then he drew his gun and walked straight to the clerk at the desk. "Give me all the money out of your safe—now."

Exposure had left him a little weary, but he managed to take the moneybag from the clerk and turn to the door without losing his ambulatory capabilities. No one in the hotel noticed the action at the desk, and no more words were spoken as John retraced his steps, remounted his horse, and set out for the wilderness again.

Over the next few days, John pushed on through the still-occasional snows. Once again, he was living off the meager offerings of the land. He was still cold and hungry, but he wasn't broke anymore. That made him feel better.

There were few distractions to keep his mind occupied, so he did a lot of remembering. Once, he even admitted to himself that the loot he stashed at the hideout was for when he and Marcia settled down together. More often, though, he remembered leaving her ranch home in a rage, and that convinced him he really had no such yearning. There could never be a lasting relationship between them. They both would have to compromise too much for the other. He told himself he was sure of that. But he only believed himself occasionally, and then it was only for short periods of time.

"The world is changing," he said aloud one night in the woods. "Why can't things just stay the way they were—just me and Al? When it was just us, before we got so big . . . oh, I don't know. I'm getting old. Everything is getting so complicated. No one used to challenge me. I made my own challenges, and now they're thrown at me."

On his lonely days of wandering, John's thoughts also drifted back toward his gang, and he wondered if he would ever see them again. He also wondered if Lan went back and retrieved the loot John had shown him. *If so, did he keep it for himself, or did he make sure Al was taken care of? I wonder how Al's doing? Lan—the outlaw who wouldn't carry a gun. He had a lot more guts than anyone else I know.*

Only Lan was permitted to stand up to John. He wasn't sure why he allowed it. But even Lan had gone too far. John well remembered the last night at the hideout, when Lan had wrestled the gun from his hand and taken charge. John had to admit that it probably saved his life, but he would never let Lan know he felt that way.

John thought about Gary too. He had always been a sore spot with John. But he had to admire Gary's brains. John owed his life to Gary too. Only he had considered escape plans. Gary did his best not to threaten John's leadership, but still, John couldn't find it in his heart to care for him.

As much as John thought about all the members of the gang who had emerged from the tunnel on the side of the hill that fall evening, he delayed heading for Carson City. During the two years it took him to ride from Wyoming to Nevada, he didn't want to think about what he would do when he arrived. That's why it took so long. Things were different. They had been driven from their kingdom. And he would have to eat a lot of crow if he didn't kill Lan for his interference. But John really didn't want to kill Lan.

No one would dare bring the conflict up to him. They wouldn't want him to act on the situation either—or would they? Things had changed, perhaps even more for them than for him. They might think they had to force him to act. The world was becoming too complicated and confusing for him.

"Where are you headed, mister?" a kid asked John as he mounted his freshly loaded horse in Garrison, Utah, along the way.

John considered ignoring him, or knocking him down, but there was a cavalry contingency there that made John reluctant to draw attention to himself. Strangely, he answered the kid. "I don't know where I'm going . . . Carson City, I guess. I'd stick around here, but I don't see any reason to."

The kid snickered. "Then you ain't seen my mom."

"Is that so? Is that so?" John simply aimed his horse west.

John wondered how long his gang would wait for him this time. He was sure the Williams Gang would never again see the glory it had seen in Wyoming. He had lost his dream. The fact that he had lived his dream for a while was not satisfactory to him. The gang that even the United States government feared to attack was no more.

The Williams Gang was not defeated, he told himself. *The men who were the gang are still alive and waiting for me in Nevada — maybe.* Even though he lied to himself, he knew they might all be dead or they might not wait for him. He also knew they might not go to Nevada, even if they did survive. Would they really fear an aging man's wrath? After all, they might think he was dead. John laughed. Maybe the law thought he was dead. It didn't seem to matter anymore.

John doubted there was any pursuit. The gang's primary enemies would be happy just to have them out of power and probably out of the territory. *Or is it a state now?* John didn't know and didn't care.

John turned fifty-six years old as he headed toward the final stretch on the way to Nevada. He was facing the foe he considered the most terrifying — age. Still, even though other outlaws might have sought comfort in their declining years, after a career of danger, John needed a few more pieces of mayhem before he could lay down the firebrand.

Feeling that strongly in his being, he worked up the courage to head for Carson City. He finally was ready to face the future, on his terms. As the paunching, middle-aged man meandered toward his destination, he smiled at the thought of his last hurrah.

The day after John's plan formed in his mind, he spent the night in a warm bed, beside a young girl, and with a full belly.

As the months passed by, the men who remained of the Williams Gang collected in Carson City.

Lan arrived first. He had no doubt that the gang still existed and that they would gather as planned. As the others arrived, he praised those who had chosen to come, which eventually meant the six leaders who had left the rimrocks in the fall two years earlier. John was the only leader missing.

Lan's path had wound southerly, to avoid the worst of the winter, but he always knew Nevada was his destination. As he was skirting through northern New Mexico and Arizona territories, he worried about whether or not the gang was still wanted in that area. He, John, and Al had stirred up trouble in Tombstone and Santa Fe—and even Colorado. Reports about Billy the Kid's death at the hands of Pat Garrett reminded Lan that many things were different. The range war was over, and forty-six years had gone into the history books since the Gadsden Purchase had added sizeable land area to the territories. But the only history on Lan's mind was the years—disconnected by spells of separation—that he had spent with the Williams brothers.

He crossed the snowy Superstition Mountains, winding his way back north and west, as spring began to break. The steep canyons flowed with water as he wound up and down the paths across them. At one point, while laid up with a sprained ankle he suffered from walking on loose scree, he wondered why he didn't just leave the past behind and head somewhere else. Surely John's flamboyant behavior would get him killed someday—and those around him as well. There was always the chance that John would hunt him down if he abandoned the gang, but that was not what kept Lan headed toward Carson City. Something else drew him to Carson City, but he didn't know what.

It was possible for Lan to live within the law. He'd done that for months after leaving Lander. He'd worked odd jobs—ranch work—and lived off the land. That was how he survived. Not once did he act out his role as an outlaw.

"It's time for me to move on," he said to the last man he worked for.

"Where are you headed?"

"I don't know. West, I guess."

Of course, being an outlaw without a gun was a difficult role to succeed in anyway. The lawmen who crossed his path showed no interest in him. It was obvious he could lead a law-abiding life that would allow him to grow old in reasonable comfort. Yet, Lan found himself inexorably drawn to Carson City. Perhaps it was John's flamboyance that drew him. Maybe it was the same sort of attraction that drew John and Marcia to each other. Maybe it was just the lack of power and prestige in being a ranch hand or a laborer of any kind—the only things Lan was cut out for, other than being in the gang. Lan believed there was future glory in his life, and he was determined to have it. That meant staying with the Williams Gang.

When he arrived in Carson City, he had found no one waiting for him. He settled into a temporary job, working in the livery stable. The stable was not unlike ones he had robbed or stolen horses from in the past.

～⊚ ⊚◟～

Gary was the second to arrive. His route hadn't been much different than Lan's. He hadn't feared passing through the southern territories because he hadn't been part of the gang when there had been trouble there. There was little likelihood of being recognized. Still, the gang was wanted, and posters had been circulated all over the West. Gary had waited into spring before crossing the divide and making it to the shadow of the Sierras.

Gary questioned his allegiance to the gang. Undoubtedly, he could do well on his own. He even had considered forming his own gang, but the time for gangs in the West was waning. He had the creativity to live any lifestyle he desired. His grudge against the Army for expelling him from West Point had spurred him to accede to Lan's wishes in Wyoming, but could that account for his traveling to rendezvous with a relationship that could cost him his life?

He enjoyed having more control than he could have had in the Army, even if he had made general. Attaining the rank of general would certainly have taken longer than his immediate rise to third-in-command of the large and powerful Williams Gang. That power had been short-lived, and of course, there was less chance of being shot by a superior while in the Army.

"I'm still mad at the Army," he had told Lan before the raid in Lander. "They had no reason to drum me out."

Now, the cavalry had routed the gang. There would be no chance to regain their former glory, unless somehow John Williams could come up with something to settle his dishonor. Gary shook his head. *I'm hoping we'll have a chance to even the score. I would have made a good officer. Now, all I want is revenge.*

Why did he intend to join with this lunatic and his followers again in Carson City? Gary could only guess it was curiosity. John might give him his only chance for satisfaction. John could make the impossible possible. *What will John be up to next?* He had to know.

Whether it was just curiosity or a lack of motivation to do anything else, Gary's desire to avenge his failure at West Point did have a place in his plans. Doubts and fears, however, kept him from getting to Carson City quickly. If delaying cost him connecting with the gang, then he could claim it wasn't his conscious decision. If he did meet with the gang . . . well, he could live with whatever circumstances he found in Nevada.

Al, of course, just wanted to see his brother. It was the only life he knew. He and John had always been together. John and the gang were the only people in Al's life. He had never been in love, had no other family, and had no reason to be anywhere but at John's side.

On his way to Nevada, Al heard stories of safes being knocked off and wondered how many of them were due to Art supporting himself in his preferred manner. It seemed the trail of reported safe cracking was moving west, and Al was pleasantly surprised that sheepish Art seemed to be heading for the rendezvous.

There were also stories of brutal beatings that were officially attributed to "a member of the Williams Gang." Al assumed some people had crossed slow-witted Les. The easy-going cook would only strike back when cornered or teased, but he had the powerful body that fit the deeds attributed to the gang member. Presumably, Les too was working his way west. He probably was cooking for ranch hands or at a café. Al knew Les would only lead the life of an outlaw if he needed more money than he could make working, and of course, years of having anything he wanted while the gang ran Lander had spoiled him.

So, at least some of the guys were working their way west. Al rode on, anxious to see John and the rest of the guys.

"Yes, I like to cook," Les said to a cowboy who was taunting him. "What of it?"

"Well, cookie, I heard only sissies and girls like to cook. Every cattle drive I've been on, the cooks were all just a little pansy-like."

Les said nothing and went on flipping pancakes.

"Now, this ain't a cattle drive. It's a nice little café with frilly curtains.

But I think you're a little pansy too, ain't ya?"

Les turned from the wood-burning range with the skillet in his hand. Before the cowboy knew what was coming, he was dead on the floor. Les removed his apron and walked permanently out the door, mumbling to himself. "Ain't no pansy. Just like cooking . . . nothing wrong with that . . . don't make enough money to stand for that kind of talk . . . gotta get to Carson."

Al had not heard news of any activity that could be attributed to Steve. He only plied his specialty, arson, when paid. So, being on the move, he wasn't likely to engage in such behavior. But, of course, Al knew that Steve could be dead. There were enough reports, however, to make it obvious that the Williams Gang was on the loose. Al only hoped the rapes and shootings he heard of were not the work of his brother.

Al felt confident that John, Lan, Art, and Gary were alive. When he reached Carson City, he was relieved to find everyone, except John. But he was confident that John was on his way. So, in the meantime, Al caught up the other guys.

Les got a job cooking in a café in town. Al joined Lan at the stables, even though he didn't exactly pull his weight. Gary and Steve made a living as a gambling team. Gary played the cards, and Steve "helped" him. Art occasionally made trips out of town to knock off a distant bank vault.

Lan had decided that no activity should draw attention to them. They would simply wait for John. Anything that would cause them to flee would interfere with that plan, so Lan would not allow it. None of the men questioned Lan's leadership, and he quickly put to rest any talk of John not showing up. Thus, life went on quietly for the outlaws. In truth, it didn't matter to them what happened. They lived one day at a time.

So much time had gone by, and such divergent paths had led the gang to Carson City, that there was no concern caused by the gang's presence in town. The law was not aware that almost the entire remnant of the Williams Gang was comfortably biding its time together in Nevada. Only six men in Carson City knew that the Williams Gang was still a singular unit.

When months turned into years, the gang settled permanently in Carson City. Only Lan was sure things would change someday. He didn't set a timeframe, but as long as there was no news of John's death or capture, he would continue to wait. If the others knew what was good for them, so would they.

⁂

"Al, I'm going to the saloon for a drink," Lan told his working partner as he left the stable. "It's been a long day and is getting dark already. I hate fall."

Lan walked into the saloon and ordered a drink. And that's when he saw John.

John, who was seated at a table, smiled at Lan.

"Well, it's about time you showed up," Lan said. "It's almost 1900, you know. It's nice you could join us before the turn of the century." Lan walked to the table where John was seated. "I was about to change the name of the gang to the Phelan Gang."

"You just try it. I still owe you one. . . . maybe more than one." John replied, wasting no sentiment on the reunion.

Lan looked toward the door as Al walked in and saw his brother.

"Where have you been?" Al's smiling face revealed his joy.

"I've been all over Utah, southern Idaho, northern Arizona, and most of Nevada," John said. "I didn't want you guys to think I was anxious to join you here. Besides, I wanted to make sure you had time to get here before me. I don't like sitting around, you know."

"I know." Al laughed.

John grimaced, and Al cut the laugh short.

⁂

"I had other reasons for taking so long too." John suddenly realized that all he had in the world was Al, and the other men of the Williams

Gang. There was nothing else he would miss when he passed from this world—not even Marcia.

Another man came into the saloon and stepped around Lan and Al as John finished his comment. "We're all here all right," Gary said. He pulled a chair away from the table and sat, facing John. "We've been meeting here at this time pretty much every day since each of us showed up. We heard reports of some crazy stunts around Nevada lately, and I figured it was you, homing in on Carson City."

"You calling me crazy again?" John asked. He picked up his chair and raised it in the air.

"Knock it off, John," Lan said. "We're not young enough to be hotheads anymore." Lan stopped. He obviously wasn't sure where he and John stood.

"I can still use a gun and outdraw you," John said.

"Yeah, since I still don't use a gun, that shouldn't be too tough."

Art wandered in the door and joined the other men. He stared at John and waited for a response. Slowly, John's hearty guffaw melted the tension.

By the time Steve made it to their usual evening gathering spot, the liquor was flowing liberally. The frivolity lasted for a while, and then the conversation turned serious.

"Some of us have been living around here for some time, waiting for you," Gary said.

John cut him off. "Les, Art, Steve—I'll to talk to these guys a minute." The lesser members of the gang knew they were not part of the tight group that got to stay at the table.

"Now that we're all together, I want to tell you about my plans . . ." John began.

Al and Lan looked at each other and shrugged. They only smiled. Years before, they might have made a bigger show of emotions.

"We are not young anymore," Al said. "It's like Lan said—"

"Still chicken, little brother?" John said. "You've been hanging around with these guys too long." John motioned toward Lan.

"He's just saying that there are young men out there who are just like we were, and we can't compete with them," Lan added. "We can't pull off any more big-time jobs. It's not just the law anymore."

Though John secretly agreed, he couldn't discard the idea he had come up with on his trip to Nevada. "Do you all plan to live the rest of your lives making an honest living?" John asked.

"It would be different if we still had the setup in Lander," Gary said. "But we don't have that. What is it you plan to do?"

John didn't respond.

≈≈

Lan jumped in. "We're starting over now, as old men." He had to disagree with John's unvoiced plans. "I have an idea that you and I should talk about in private. I know how we can set ourselves up to live our lives comfortably and peacefully."

John scowled at Lan. "Who wants to live peacefully? We're going back to Wyoming." John looked around, obviously waiting for a reaction. "I want the Williams Gang to go out on a vengeful note. I want to go to Wyoming and raze Lander."

The men knew it was useless to argue. They left the saloon one at a time. Art, Les, and Steve didn't know the details but had heard John's louder exclamations.

Lan knew that part of the reason John wanted to go back was the loot in the basin hideout. But that knowledge would not be shared with the others, not even Al. Given his lack of choice, Lan thought the loot was a worthy enough reason for going back. He had seen little of it, but he was impressed with the staggering value of what else must be left in the hole. His own idea for comfort would be unnecessary.

Lan also wondered if Marcia played a part in John's plans. There was no way to ask, but Lan knew they were about to find out.

≈≈

Lan approached John at dinner the next night. It was time to explore as many of John's intentions as was safely possible.

"I plan to use some of the money in the pit to buy the things we need to destroy Lander," John said. "We'll get things like dynamite, rifles, ammunition, and anything that burns. I figure we can sneak in, get the loot, and set out to round up the stuff we need far enough from Lander to avoid causing a panic. I don't want them having any advance warning, so we can't just steal the stuff and cause a ruckus. Whatever is left of the stash, I'll split among the seven of us. When we break up, we'll be fixed for the remainder of our days."

Lan understood that the money would be the lure to keep the gang heading for Lander. John would inform the men what he had for them if they went through with his plans and thus insure their loyalty.

There had been no mention of Marcia, so Lan could only assume she was not part of John's plan for vengeance. But he would wait and see.

"John, why is it so important to wreak havoc on Lander?" Lan asked. "Why do you hate the town so much?"

"The people in that town had a good life under us. But they weren't happy. They undermined us at every chance. Their statehood plans were so important. They chased us before we took over; they fought against us when we ran the town. They sent lawmen after us at the hideout and finally persuaded the cavalry to come after us. They eventually got someone to infiltrate the hideout and nearly killed us all. Why do I hate Lander?"

Lan took a bite of food and contemplated what John said. "Not everybody was against us, John. Besides, there are a lot of people there now who weren't there then. You also have to realize that we were outlaws. Most of the campaign against us was the work of that sheriff—Swift. Why not just find him?"

"There won't be any Lander when I get done," John growled. "The Williams Gang will be the ruin of central Wyoming."

It took them only a few days to get started. The tale of the loot John would split with them convinced the men to follow John's trail one final time.

Only one day out, that resolve began to fray at the edges.

"What kind of idiot do you think I am?" Les asked.

"You agreed to come along on this final raid," Lan said.

"Yeah, under threat to my life."

"That threat still stands, Les."

"I've been thinking it over. John's the only one who would shoot me for running. You couldn't if you wanted to. All I have to do is pick my time."

"You know he would come after you," Lan said. The two men were riding side by side, quietly chatting while the others rode slightly ahead of them.

"Not while he's all excited about going back to Lander. By the time his party's over, he would never be able to find me."

"Well, I'll give you a choice, Les. I can tie you up the rest of the way, knock you out whenever I have to, or you can give me your word you won't desert."

"You would accept my word?"

"Yes."

"I would have to say that's new for me—someone trusting my word. But I mainly think you're a fool, Lan Phelan, a fool to trust my word and a fool to be a part of the Williams Gang."

"I've lived a pretty good life as a part of the Williams Gang. You have too. You haven't been lacking anything while we've been together. Did you like your job in Carson City better? You're an outlaw. One way or the other, you chose this life. John's made it pay off for you, whatever his faults are."

"You recruited me, not him."

"But I recruited you for him, and I told you what to expect. You agreed to come along because the offer was better than what you had. Now, do I have your word to keep that agreement or don't I?"

Just then, a commotion broke out on the trail in front of them.

"What the?" Les said.

John's horse broke through the brush at a full gallop, barely preceded by a frightened rabbit.

"Hyah!" John said as he spurred his horse. "Dinner!"

Lan's question went unanswered.

BADMAN, Polzin

A couple of days later, the gang was subsisting on food from the land for the umpteenth time and tired of it. They were making slow progress toward Wyoming, and John was feeling a sense of adventure again.

"We need to raid a ranch or something," John said. "We can steal some real food, or better yet, we can have a ranch wife serve us up some home cooking."

"We don't want to cause a ruckus," Lan said. "Any attention we draw to a group of men moving across the country and stealing or robbing will alert the authorities that we're still together. Then they'll wonder where we're headed, and then . . ."

"Yeah, yeah, I know."

They finally made town one evening, and John found himself using his last few coins in a poker game that netted him not only some monetary gains but also attached another young gun to the gang.

"You interested in a little excitement?" John asked the tough-looking, young man. "What's your name?"

"Wyatt." The kid looked up from his hand and looked John straight in the eyes. "What do you have in mind? You can't be calling me a cheater. You're doing all the winning. So I don't think you're planning any gun play."

"No. No." John put the man at ease. "You ever heard of the Williams Gang?"

"Weren't they a big deal a few years ago? I hear they're all dead now. I haven't heard anything about them for a long time."

"I'm John Williams. We're not dead."

"Oh." The kid's bravado sank. He obviously remembered the ruthlessness attributed to John Williams.

"Relax, kid. I'm asking you if you would like to join up with us. We're on our way to make a big killing in Wyoming. We need men like you—young, looking for something more in their lives."

Lan wandered up, hearing John pronounce their identity. "John," Lan said.

"Don't worry, Lan. This young man is going to be our newest gang member. Either that or he's going to be dead soon. He won't be telling any secrets."

The kid began to sweat. He slowly stood up from his chair.

"Well, what do you say kid?" John asked. "You with us or dead?"

The kid smiled. That was enough of an answer for John.

The trek across Nevada, then Utah, took about a month. Along the way, they gathered some stolen goods and enough new men to bring the gang to thirty-five members. Attention was avoided successfully until they were not far from Lander.

"I'm bored, boys," John said. "Look at this quiet, little town here. It's just too peaceful."

"We're too close to Lander and reaching our goal now to draw any attention to ourselves," Lan said. "People are already noticing this large group of men moving across the land. We want to take Lander and Sheriff Swift by surprise. Causing a ruckus won't help."

"Aw, a little harmless fun won't hurt anything," John said. He nudged his horse forward at a walk, then a trot, and then a gallop. "Hyah!" he screamed . . . to the town, not the horse.

Lan and the others were forced to follow.

"I'll bet there's some women in that saloon, Lan."

"Don't do this." Lan yelled.

But John pulled up his horse at the saloon's hitching rail and jumped off. Before Lan and the others could dismount, John was through the doorway and making a beeline for a woman wearing a blue dress, who was sitting in a gambler's lap.

John grabbed the woman's arm and pulled her to her feet without a word.

"Hey," the woman and the poker player both said at the same time.

"I've got a hankering for a little rough loving, woman," John said. "How about you?"

The man sitting at the table with his mouth open started to get up.

"Don't bother, George," the woman said. "This man sounds like he's ready to spend some money on something besides cards. That suits me just fine."

"I wasn't planning on paying for anything," John said.

"We'll see about that," she said. She took his hand off her arm and wrapped it around her waist. Then she walked him away from the table. "My name's Mae. I run this place. What's your name?"

"John."

Lan was watching the room for danger signs but saw none.

"Looks like I'll be busy for a while," John said to the gang. "You fellows fend for yourselves."

The outlaws knew the routine. They set out for the bar, poker tables, and back out the door, as their preferences directed them.

"Here we go again," Lan said to Al. But he knew there was nothing he could do, and he was glad it was no worse than it was.

"You boys ready?" John asked the men as they prepared their horses for the ride. "I want to stop short of the basin and do some looking around before we commit to occupying it. Let's see where we end up tonight."

They made camp outside the rimrocks, despite the objections of Gary and the others. John insisted that he and Lan would take their time scouting the basin for activity that could prove dangerous to them. The men believed they would be safer inside the bowl. They feared that their presence had been noted and that setting up for the night outside the bowl might draw attention. But as night arrived, they made camp and accepted John's explanation of the need for scouting.

Of course, the real reason for the caution was to provide an opportunity for John and Lan to dig up the hidden loot inside the bowl in private. John had no intention of letting the men turn on him at the last minute and take the money and stolen goods. They could be aware of its presence but not of its location. They had to be kept waiting until John decided to divvy it up.

Lan and John made their way to the still-discernible stack of rocks that guarded the treasure. Though a trap was unlikely, the two men moved cautiously. The two gang leaders also were aware that someone from the gang might follow them and learn the secret and that the authorities knew they likely weren't all dead and that the gang could return to the hideout someday. Thus, they moved guardedly and scoured the surroundings for movement or sounds, just to be sure, before they began removing the boulders and rocks.

"Well, there's been a bit of dust stirred up in here," John said, indicating the cannoned rubble. "The lean-tos are flattened. But the basin hasn't changed much."

Lan set a rock aside. "A few pieces of the trail are missing, and some of the rocks have found new places to settle." He was nervous and not sure why. He looked across the distance to the old camp. "I bet there's a lot of bullet holes in those old boards, judging by the way it sounded when we left." He shuddered, remembering what had nearly happened to them a decade earlier. "I wonder how many of the young guys survived? I never heard about arrests or anything."

John continued pulling stones off the stack, uncovering the first pocket of loot. Then in the fall, post-dusk darkness, John lifted something from the ground.

"Is that gold dust?" Lan surveyed the sack in John's hands.

"Yeah. And here's a bag of watches, necklaces, and other jewelry." He looked into another bag. I got this stuff before I learned cash was easier to carry." John was obviously enjoying himself, reliving past glories. "I didn't realize you and I had taken so much out of here. I put these here a long time ago."

They continued to retrieve the loot, and with each passing moment, Lan's nervousness grew. Each bag of money, each trinket, brought back memories for John, and he spent time dwelling over them. Lan didn't need to hear the stories. He just wanted to get the loot and get out of there.

"Ah, here's the first bag of gold I put in here. I was just a kid when I found this hideout. Sure, others have been in here, but no one ever discovered this hole." Uncharacteristic words suddenly came out of John. "Lan, I'm fifty-six years old. I probably wouldn't have lived this long if it weren't for you . . . thanks." John put his hand on Lan's arm.

Lan looked at John's hand and squeezed it firmly. He reflected on his longtime relationship with this man. *How many years ago did we meet?* He still remembered that day he was lured away from a river empty of fish and a peaceful life. "Well, John, my life would probably have been awfully dull without you," Lan said. "So, let's call it even."

The softness was gone from John's voice when he spoke again. "We'll get our vengeance on Lander, and then I'll retire and live to a ripe, old age. That's what you want me to do, isn't it? I promise I'll do it." John laughed at the top of his lungs. Then, he turned from the hole and began loading his saddlebags with the loot.

Lan didn't think John had meant a word he'd said, even the thanks for saving his life. "You know there's something I've wanted to tell you for years now."

"What's that?"

"Well, it's possible that Les kept some of the loot he and the young ones rounded up before the battle here."

"What?"

"John, you've got to promise me to let it go. If I mean anything to you, or ever have, let it go. Promise me."

"If he thinks he can get away with—"

"John, promise."

"Oh, alright. I thought something was haywire. His take was awful skimpy. I must really be getting old. Let's get out of here."

⚜

Over the next few days, the gang scrounged the area for the necessary items to raze Lander—paying for them with the proceeds from the recovered loot. Buying things galled John, but he knew that when the time came, revenge would be worth the indignity.

Al approached his brother after one of their forays. "I've decided to set out on my own after the raid."

"We've never been separated, except for getting away from the law," John said. "How would you make it on your own?"

"I don't know. But I think it's time to give it a try. Don't try to stop me." Al's posture showed his determination.

⚜

A week later, Al saw his brother and Lan picking their way down the side of the rocky hill. That stirred the rest of the gang to their feet. It was time.

They broke camp, and by the time Lan and John joined them, they were ready to roll. They would strike at night, so they left in the early evening. The terror of fire by night far surpassed that of the same in daylight. John wanted the terror of terrors to be unleashed upon Lander.

He only regretted he couldn't somehow include the cavalry regiment in his last hurrah.

As they approached town, the gang banded together before the onslaught.

"Alright. Get that flammable stuff spread out on the wagon," John said. "Pile everything else on the other wagon. I want another wagon empty. You'll see why later."

Gary supervised the work of the younger boys. And in a few minutes, the final entry into Lander was underway.

"Alright, little brother," John said to Al. "You look me up in Nevada if you ever need anything. I'm not going to let you disappear from my life. Maybe we can talk more later."

"There won't be any time later," Al said. "My mind's made up. I've been thinking about it for a long time. I want to do something else with my life. Maybe I'll find a woman. I don't know. I'll just have to see what happens. There'll be no more talking about it for me." Al rode away from his brother.

John couldn't suppress a proud snicker. "My little brother is his own man." John found himself near Art. "What are you going to do with your share of the loot?"

Art moved away without answering.

He was saved from John's wrath by Steve stepping his horse alongside and volunteering an answer. "I'm going a long ways away from here," Steve said.

John turned to Lan, who was on John's left. "Lan, we've been together a long time. Remember when Al and I found you fishing in that stream?"

"I remember it well. We had a bunch of close calls over the years, didn't we?"

"A lot of fun is how I remember it, and a lot of money. We'll soon have more. Then, we'll go our separate ways." John paused and then went on. "You never did tell me what you're going to do."

"I was thinking . . . why not just let all the others keep everything they can get in Lander? You and I can keep what's left of the hideout loot. That way, when we take off, we won't have to spend any time dividing everything while someone might be after us."

"Yeah, sure, fine. Now, answer my question. What are you going to do afterward?"

"Well, I considered not telling you, so you won't come looking for me when you get bored. But I suppose you would find me anyway." Lan turned to face John. "I think I'll go back to Montana. I didn't get to see much of it the last time I was there." He chuckled. "I'll decide what I'm going to do once I get there. What are you planning to do in Nevada?"

"I've got it all figured out." There was a gleam in John's eyes again. "I'm going to get me a piece of Nevada land that I saw. It would make a good ranch. The folks there didn't look upon me as an outlaw, so they'll leave me alone. They don't know I'm *the* John Williams. I've got enough money. I can buy the land and some stock. I guess I finally realized I'm getting old. It's the kind of thing Marcia . . ."

"I understand," Lan said. "Why don't you go find her? Like you said, it's the kind of thing she's always wanted you to do. Can you live with yourself if you don't give it a try?"

"It doesn't matter what she wants. I'm not giving her a chance to turn me in again." John looked away. "Besides, she might not be alive." He didn't want to think about that. "I'm going to work that ranch for myself. I'll hire a couple of hands, but I'm going to be the one who gets to enjoy it—all by myself. It'll be for me." John pounded his fist into his hand.

⚜

Lan thought it was a shame. John had forced himself to abandon something that might have given him the satisfaction that had always eluded him.

"One more thing I'm going to do," John continued. "I'm going to buy into a saloon out there. As the West tames down, people will still want a place to go to break loose. I intend to give them that place. Too many old lady ideas are already creeping out here from the East. The newer trains are faster, which makes them too hard to rob." He chuckled. "And gas lights are getting too common — not enough darkness to sneak around in anymore. Even in California, some of the cities have them. I even heard of something called a horseless carriage."

Lan had never heard John talk like this. He stayed quiet, hoping John would go on. He did.

"My place is going to be old-fashioned, both the ranch and the saloon. I'm going to hang on to what's left of the good old days, if I can. I spent some time talking to people on my way out to meet you guys. I think Nevada is going to be the place to be. There's still some silver out there, and who knows what else? I don't hanker to be a miner, and I'm too old to steal it anymore, but I want to help relieve those people who do mine it and steal it of their silver."

A lizard crawled from under a rock. John quickly drew his gun and shot it. He laughed as the lizard flew in the air and then hit the ground in a mangled heap. It was amazing that John had even seen it in the darkness. Lan looked at John and knew he hadn't changed much.

At the edge of town, the entire gang began whooping and yelling. The men rode through the main street and sent the townsfolk scattering. They lit the fire in the tanker wagon, and they released the teams of horses at full gallop. The first wagon careened into a store window and soon lit up the street. They lit another wagon, and it crashed through the window of the little café John had spent hours in during the occupation. The building caught fire.

The wagon loaded with all the other flammables and explosives careened down the street and flip-flopped, end over end, finally coming to rest at the door of the sheriff's office. Two people ran out of the office and collided with the wagon, catching their clothing on fire. One of the people was wearing a simple, blue dress. When John saw her, pain hit his chest. *Marcia often wore a dress like that.* John realized Marcia could be in town. He rode down the street toward the woman. He had to know.

The woman tore her skirt from her body to escape the flames. John rode his horse madly past her. It wasn't Marcia. He intentionally knocked the woman down as he passed, angry that it wasn't Marcia, but glad it wasn't.

The gang ran through the town and then turned and rode back the other way, shooting everyone who came into their view. The dynamite exploded precariously where it had spilled from its wagon.

The outlaws gave no thought to the possibility of return fire from the residents of the town. They also had no concern for the horses that were hitched to the wagons. John took joy in shooting any moving target that was not part of his gang—young or old, male or female, animal or human, it didn't matter to him.

The outlaws doubled back and passed through the town a second time. Some of the gang ran into the buildings that weren't yet aflame and helped themselves to anything worth taking. The outlaws filled the empty booty wagon quickly. It was soon overflowing with goods from the stores, the bank, and the hotel. After they chased anyone cowering inside out into the street, Steve threw sticks of dynamite into the buildings.

Eventually, someone somewhere fired at the outlaws, resulting in the death of the person defending property or family. Bodies littered the street. A few of them were the young men of the gang. Remnants of the buildings tumbled as the supports gave way to the flames. And through it all, John's laughter could be heard over the roaring of the flames, the firing of the guns, and the screams. The other outlaws eventually joined in, shrieking as they got into the spirit of destruction. They continued to shoot townspeople as they fled the burning buildings.

The Williams Gang made one last sweep of the town of Lander. Not a building was untouched by the fire. The resident sheriff never appeared. If he was in the flaming office, that was where he remained.

Gary rode to John's side. "OK, you've done what you wanted to do. Now, let's get out of here."

Any doubt of John's sanity was erased in the next moment.

John was caught up in the fiery destruction and beyond rationality. "You've told me what to do once too often," John said. He turned his gun on Gary and shot him through the heart. Gary fell from his horse, and John galloped away.

The other gang members rode out of town at a full gallop and went to their prearranged gathering spot. When they arrived, they missed Gary.

"Where's Gary?" Al asked.

Everyone shook their heads and lowered their eyes as probability sank in.

"He must not have made it," John said. "He was right beside me."

The men didn't pause long in their mourning. They had to get away before any retaliation was mounted from possible survivors. They gathered items from the wagon, and then two youngsters took off with the wagon and whatever was left on it. The rest of the gang mounted their horses and began to disburse.

Al rode up beside his brother.

John grinned and put his hand on Al's shoulder. "Best of luck, little brother. Hope you find a real good woman."

Al grinned back and grasped John's shoulder. "Thanks, John—for everything." He turned and rode off.

Lan reined his horse northward; John turned his to the south.

Lan wondered if he'd ever see any of them again. He raised his hand in farewell and then turned to look at John.

John touched his hat.

"Good-bye, John," Lan said.

"Good luck," John replied. Then he wiped his eyes with his lean and rugged hand and nudged his horse into a gallop. "Hyah!"

John's shout, followed by his manic laugh, was the last sound the gang heard from its leader.

The End

BADMAN, Polzin

AUTHOR'S NOTE

It is my hope that readers will enjoy the unexpected ending's deviance from books where the good guys always win. Hopefully, there is enough meat to the story to make it satisfying without it following the stereotypical outcome.

Perhaps there will be other books called *Outlaw* and *Lawman* to make those desiring a more satisfying ending more content if this book's ending didn't accomplish that. One can only hope . . .

BADMAN, Polzin